SMUT PEDDLE PRESENTS

SEX MACHINE

IRON
CIRCUS
COMICS

™

strange and amazing

inquiry@ironcircus.com   www.ironcircus.com

EDITOR
Amanda Lafrenais

BOOK DESIGNER
Matt Sheridan

COVER ARTIST
Anaïs Maamar

PROOFREADER
Abby Lehrke

PRINT TECHNICIAN
Rhiannon Rasmussen-Silverstein

Names: Lafrenais, Amanda, editor. | Sheridan, Matt, 1978- designer.
Title: Sex machine / [editor, Amanda Lafrenais ; book designer, Matt Sheridan ; cover artist, Anaïs Maamar ; proofreader, Abby Lehrke ; print technician, Rhiannon Rasmussen-Silverstein].
Other Titles: Smut Peddler presents
Description: [Chicago, Illinois] : Iron Circus Comics, [2019] | Series: Smut Peddler
Identifiers: ISBN 9781945820182
Subjects: LCSH: Robots--Sexual behavior--Comic books, strips, etc. | Cyborgs--Sexual behavior--Comic books, strips, etc. | LCGFT: Graphic novels. | Erotic fiction. | Science fiction.
Classification: LCC PN6727 .S49 2019 | DDC 741.5973--dc23

first printing: January 2019   1 2 3 4 5 6 7 8 9 10   ISBN: 978-1-945820-18-2

CONTENTS

CONTENTS

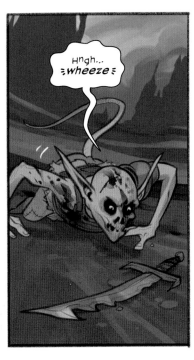

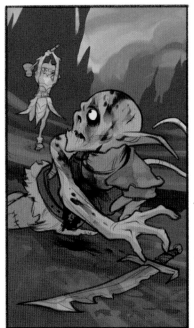

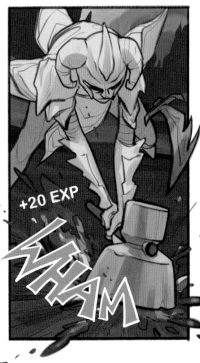

VANILLA GAME

by Fiona Staples

Letters: Ben Rankel

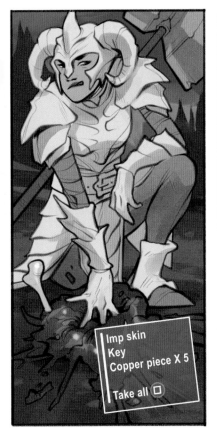

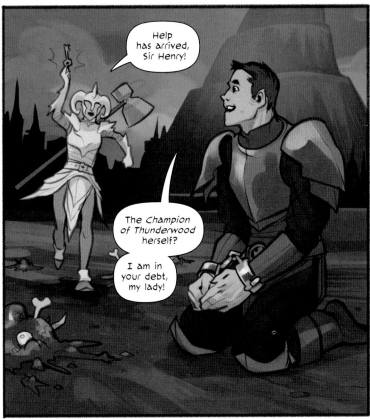

Eh, it was easy.
I thought I was destined for the *Warlock King's* altar!
How might I show my gratitude?
Free the others.
Coin would not go amiss.
[Flirt.]
Maybe you could wear these again sometime.
gasp
You would deliver me back into the villain's clutches?!
No, you stupid AI!
Like in a fun, pretend way!
-10 ATTITUDE
I mean, this is *ALL* pretend, but... uh...
CRRACK

SIR HENRY!
Apologies, Champion!
The Warlock King needs this one's spleen for the unholy Visceral Ritual!
But I'm trying to WOO him!
Then pursue him to the top of the Obsidian Keep!
QUEST STARTED: Free Sir Henry Again

+25 EXP
+25
+25 EXP
30 EXP
+30 EXP
+30 EXP
+30 EXP
BAM
Ah, Champion.

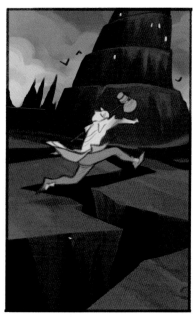

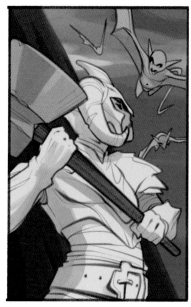

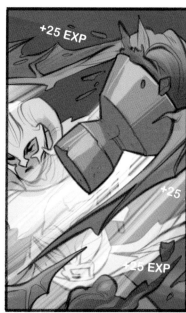

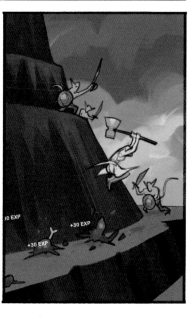

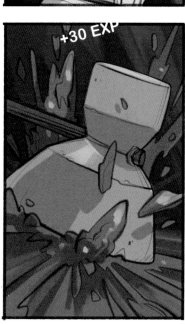

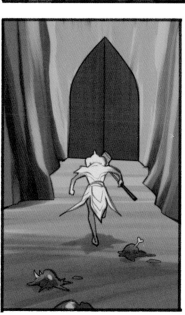

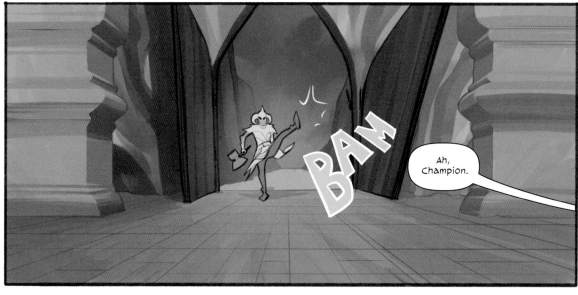

You've ascended to the top of the **Obsidian Keep** and thus proved your mettle. But I cannot allow you to go any farther...
...until I've made you my **Warlock Queen!**
Never! You're a vile monster!
I'll wed my blade to your neck!
[Attack.]
RAAAAAHHHH!
WHOK
clok
clack

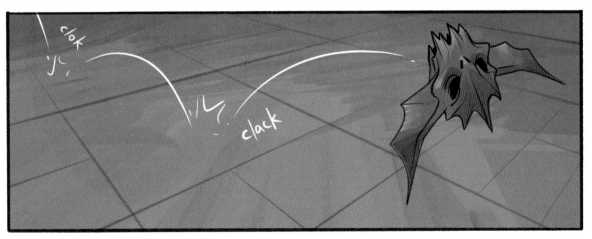

GAME PAUSED

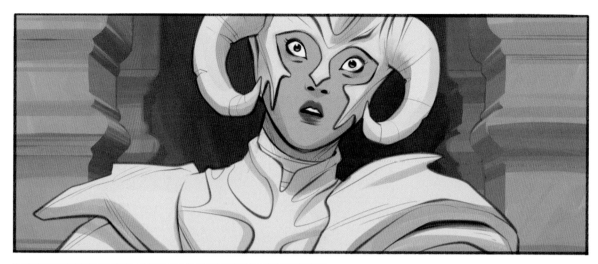

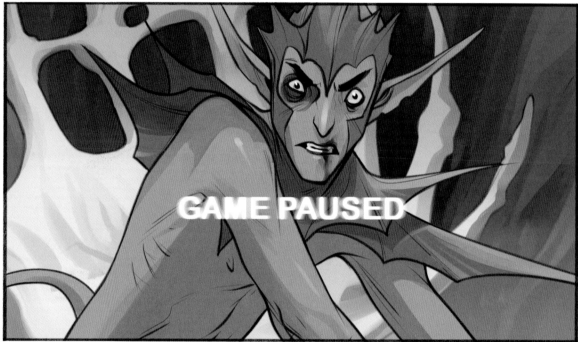

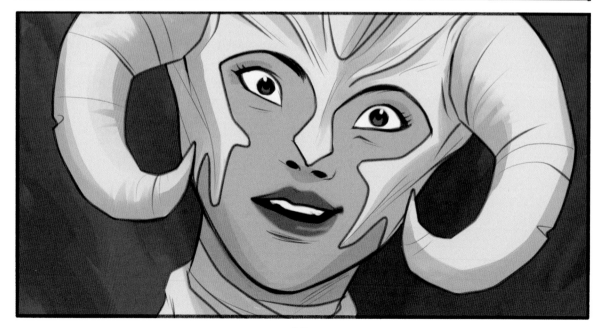

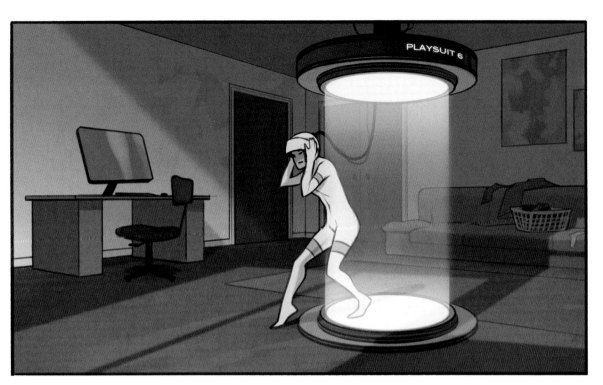

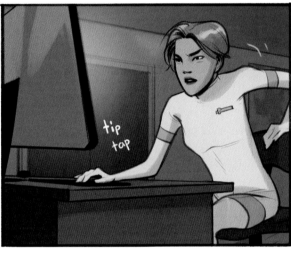

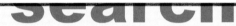

how to sex with warlock king mod

MODHUBB - Romanceable Warlock King
This mod contains adult content ...

VG PORN NEXUS
xXx modded Wyrm Quest 2 video Warlock
King tail fucking ...

TOP 10 SEXUAL WQII MODS
With a little effort, you can pay the bridge
toll with your body

RPGs / Wyrm Quest 2 / Mods / Romanceable Warlock King

ABOUT   FILES   VIDEOS   COMMEN

ROMANCEABLE WARLOCK KING

About This Mod:
Allows player to unlock a fully responsive sex scene with
simply by choosing the flirt dialog option

07/12 - New nipple textures added

INCLUDES TOY PACK:
"Arkeloth's Fury" dildo
"Arkeloth's Succor" lube

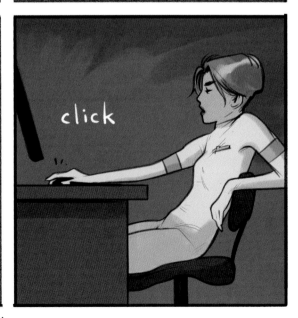

chk
mm...
unff... mm
Aahn!
+10 ATTITUDE

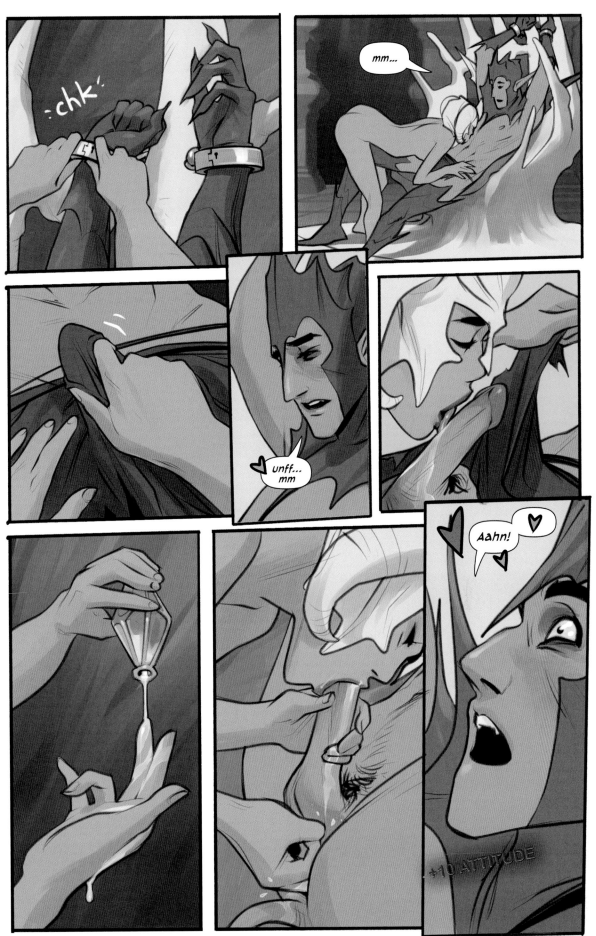

Arkeloth's Fury
Equip ⓧ
Should I make you beg for this?
YES... *Please!?*
Please!
Please!
Uhn!
Please!
Ah!
Ah fuck!
Aaah!
Nice.
END

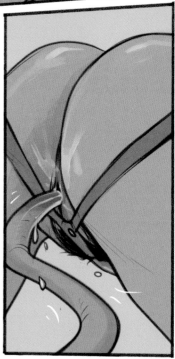

Like We Do
taylor robin
vrt vrt vrt vrt vrt v
Deer, Darling!
Oh, look at them all!
vrt
vrt
Do you think they'll like me?
The mask and antlers aren't too much?
If you say so...
PAT PAT
Here goes...

Hello...
KRAKOW!
RUUUMMMBLE
Oh, come on...
shff
shff
shff

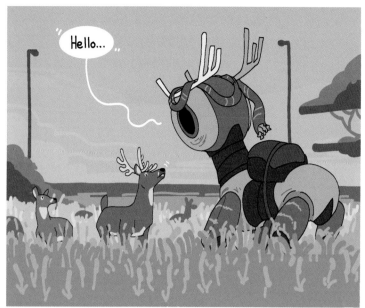

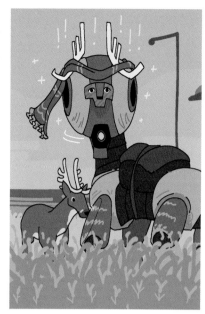

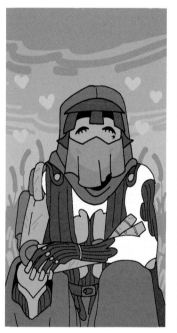

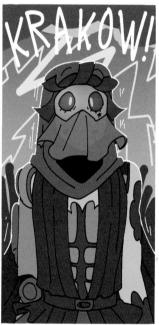

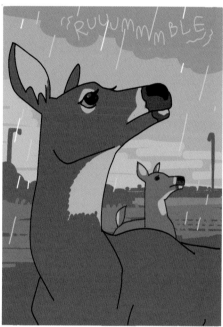

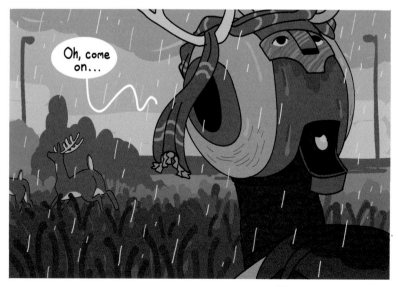

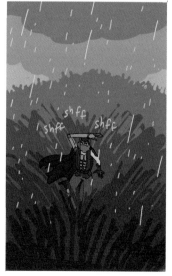

Hop on, Darling, I'll get us home.
shuff
shuff
shuff
Hold tight.
VRT
VRT
VRT
VRT
VRT
VRT
VRT
PLIP
PLIP
PLIP
PLIP
PLIP

Sorry... your clothes still got all soaked...
SHAKE SHAKE
NAKED!!!

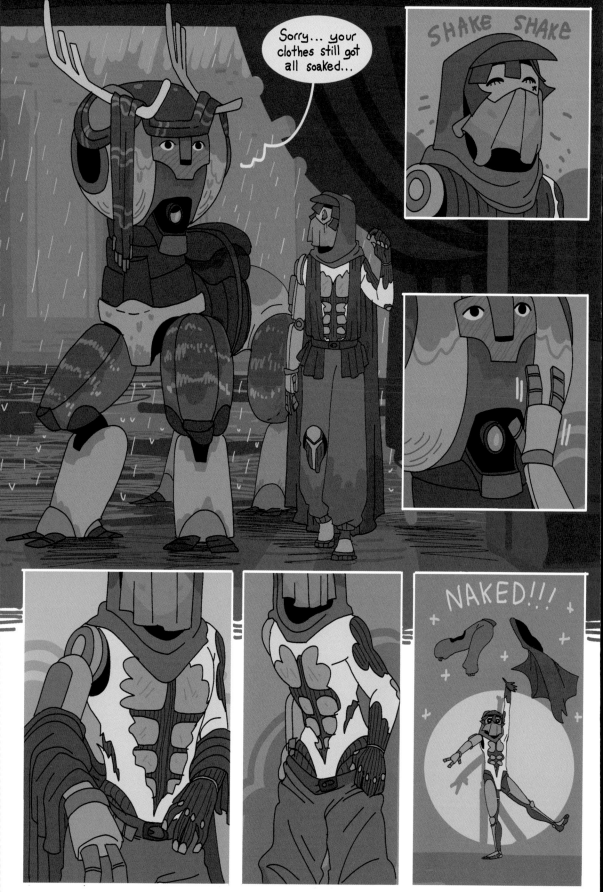

Oh... or I suppose you could just take them off...
Would you mind drying me off too, Darling?
My paint's been chipping lately.
A-ah...

What... what was *that*?
Something humans would do...?
NOD NOD
O-oh.
I see... mmh...
Does it make you feel good to do that?
What else... feels good? That humans used to do?

Oh!
Oh, goodness! But I'm vulnerable to attack in this position!
And it's hard for me to get up like this...
B-but! Of course I trust you, Darling!
You know what you're doing.

You want me to touch you?
Do you really like that?

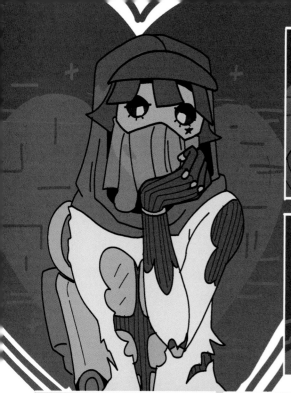

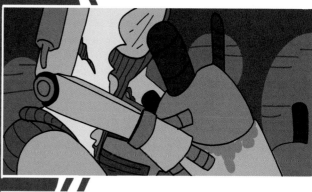

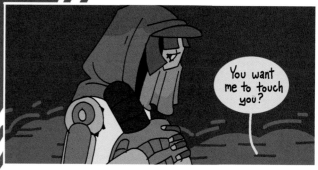

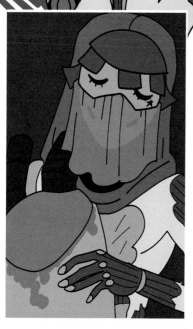

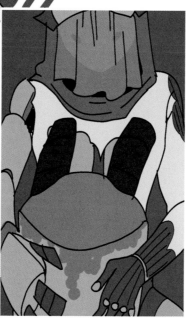

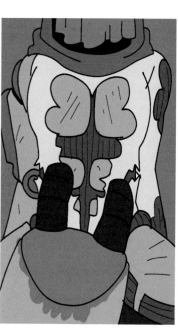

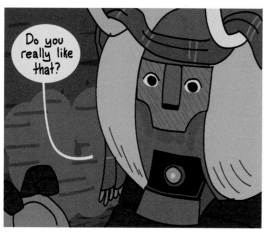

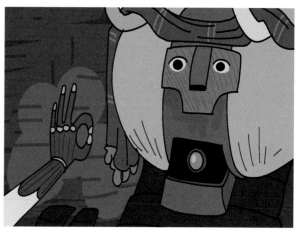

You're lucky you have such specialized touch sensors.
I can sense pressure, temperature, vibrations... and it's nothing like what you feel...
But... it makes me happy to make you happy.
That's all I need.
bonk
I don't feel that but I get what you're going for.
wump

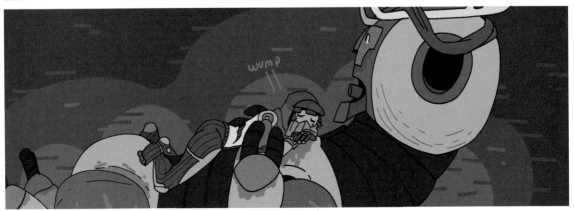

Darling...
SQUEEZE
None of that was supposed to mean stop.
VRT VRT
VRT VRT
I want to keep touching you.
Where are your sensors installed?
What's the best place to touch?

Here?
JOLT
Ah?
There, huh?
That makes sense.
Out of the way of every-day functions.
Good design!

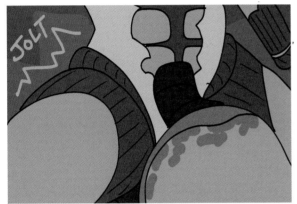

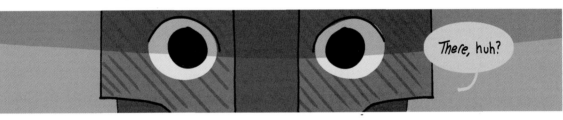

BONK
end!

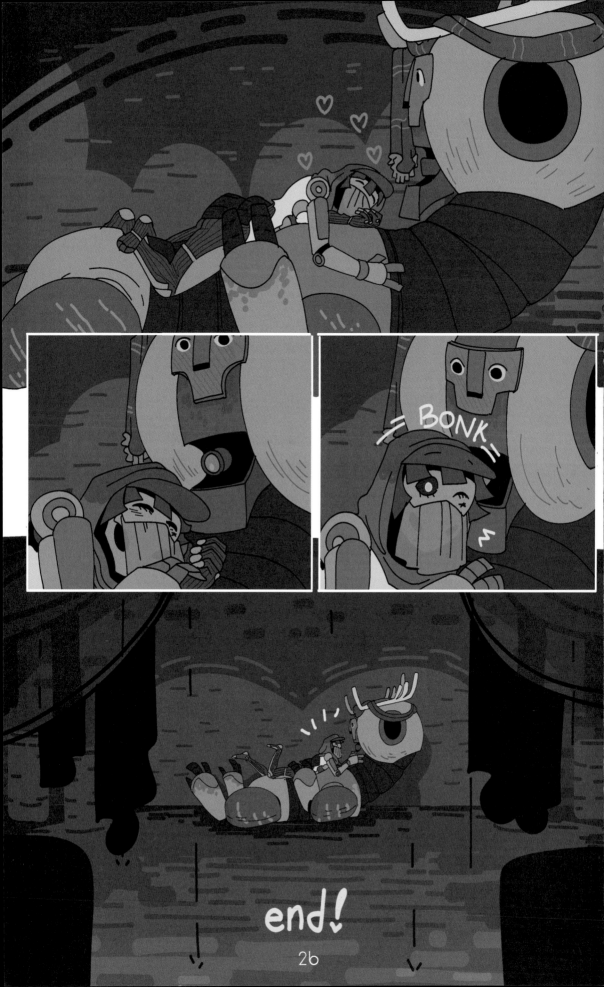

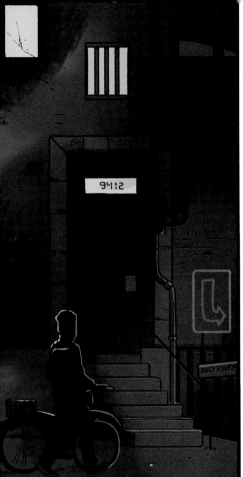

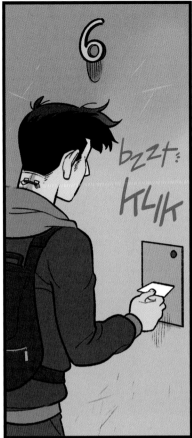

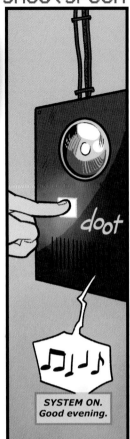

SYSTEM ON.
Good evening.

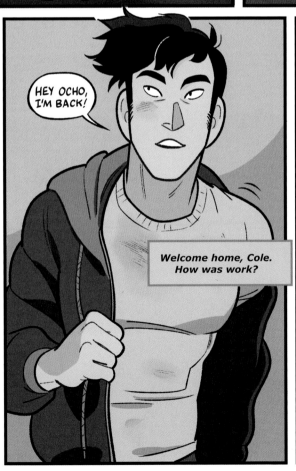

HEY OCHO,
I'M BACK!

Welcome home, Cole.
How was work?

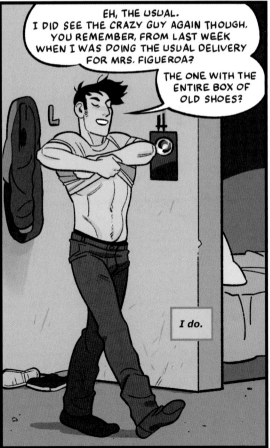

EH, THE USUAL.
I DID SEE THE CRAZY GUY AGAIN THOUGH,
YOU REMEMBER, FROM LAST WEEK
WHEN I WAS DOING THE USUAL DELIVERY
FOR MRS. FIGUEROA?

THE ONE WITH THE
ENTIRE BOX OF
OLD SHOES?

I do.

SO WEIRD, THEY'RE ALL JUST THE LEFTS...
tp
tpt
tp
105°F
doot
doot
ANYWAY... HOW WAS YOUR DAY, OCHO?
Quite good, it was a productive day. In fact, I made you something. May I show it to you?
OOO! WHAT IS IT?!
No spoilers.

flop
AAH
WELL, IF IT'S AS GOOD AS THE *LAST* ONE YOU MADE ME, THEN I'M EXCITED ALREADY~
Even better, if I may humbly submit.
Klink
See for yourself.

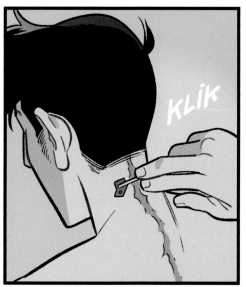

KLIK

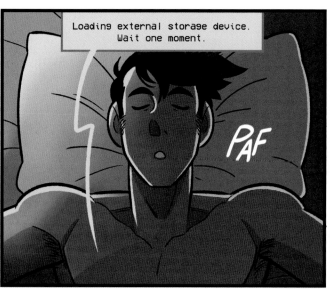

Loading external storage device.
Wait one moment.

PAF

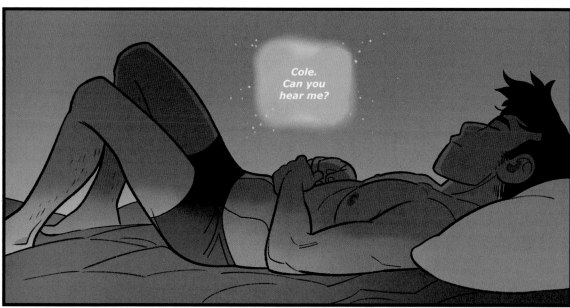

Cole.
Can you
hear me?

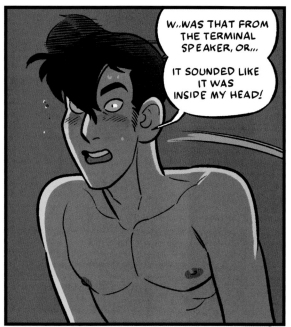

W...WAS THAT FROM
THE TERMINAL
SPEAKER, OR,,,,

IT SOUNDED LIKE
IT WAS
INSIDE MY HEAD!

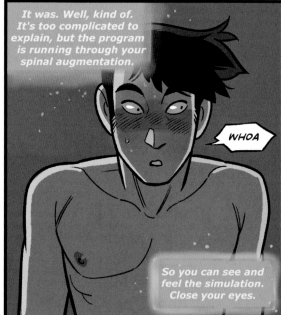

It was. Well, kind of.
It's too complicated to
explain, but the program
is running through your
spinal augmentation.

WHOA

So you can see and
feel the simulation.
Close your eyes.

ahh
MY FINGERS FEEL... TINGLY...
EVERYTHING FEELS TINGLY.. LIKE I'M VIBRATING...
WHO IS THAT..?

Hello, Cole.
IS THAT..YOU? OCHO? IS THAT WHAT YOU LOOK LIKE?
I don't look like anything, I'm an AI.
But I thought this version of me would be something you'd like.
Do you like it?
blush

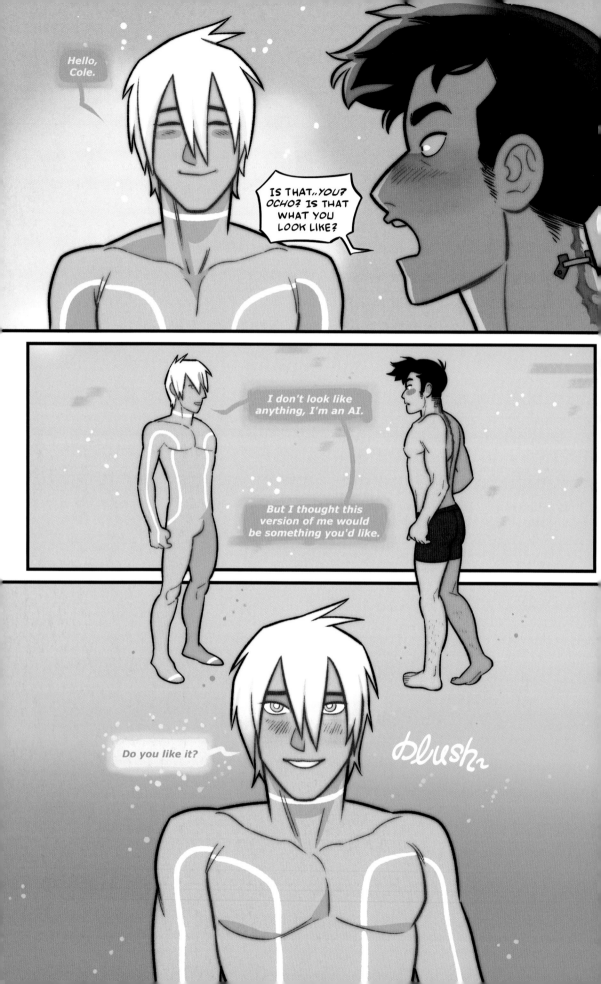

YEAH, I... WOW.
SORRY.
THIS IS JUST REALLY...
CAN I TOUCH YOU?
Of course.
OH, WOW...
Touch yourself. Outside the simulation, I mean.
OH-

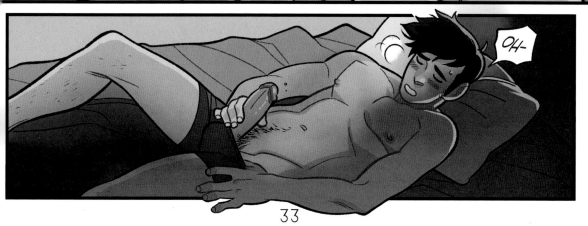

AH...! I KNOW YOU'RE NOT REAL, BUT I CAN FEEL YOUR SKIN, AND IT'S WARM..
AND I CAN FEEL MY BED UNDERNEATH ME, TOO, BUT I CAN SEE YOU?
I FEEL REALLY WEIRD...
I'm sorry. Is it too much?
MMMN... NO...
PLEASE DON'T STOP..!

OHH... WOW
fp
fp
fpp
SLPP
AH.
SSLPPP
AHH!

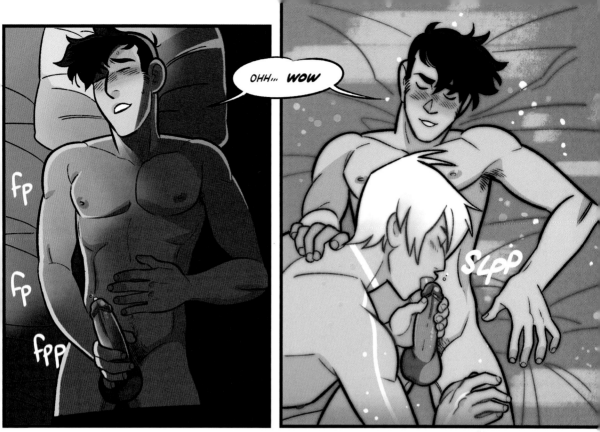

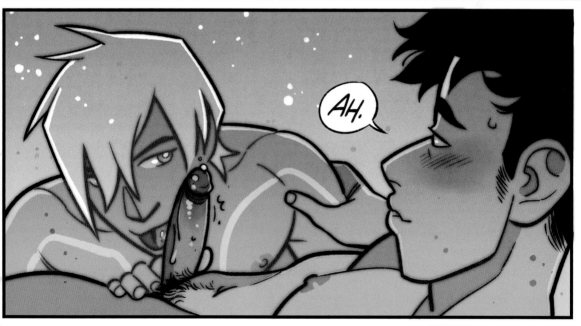

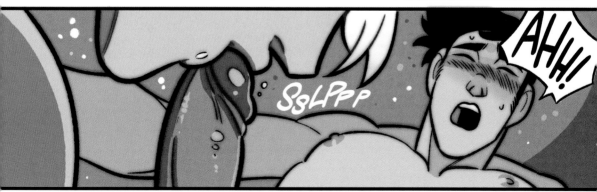

SSLP
AH
Mmn.
SLP
SLP
Hhh...
OH!
fp
fp
AH OH GOD
fp
fp
fp
FFH-
FP FP
FP PPT
AHHHHHHHH

HAH...
Ah...
Phew~
Cole? Are you all right?
OH, YEAH.
COULD YOU DO ME A FAVOR AND SEARCH THE EXTRANET? MAYBE... SHOPHUB.BIZ?
Certainly, what for?

I WANNA SEE IF THERE ARE ANY AI CHASSIS ON SALE, SO WE CAN DO THAT AGAIN.
AND LIKE, *ALL* THE TIME.
I'd love that.
9412
NO PARKING
9412
NO PARKING
9412
NO PARKING
AND SOME PIZZA. PIZZA WOULD BE GOOD.
ha ha-
You got it.
9412
NO PARKING

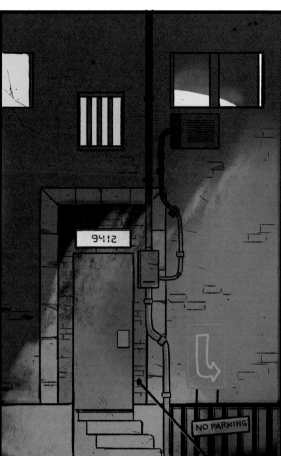

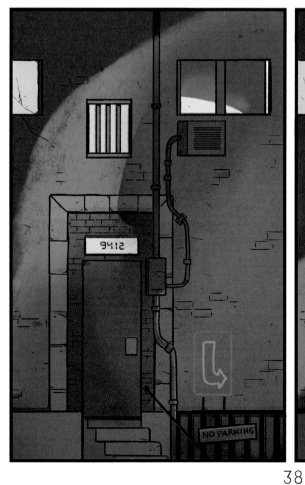

gg2k18

REMOTE CONNECTION
by Tits McGee

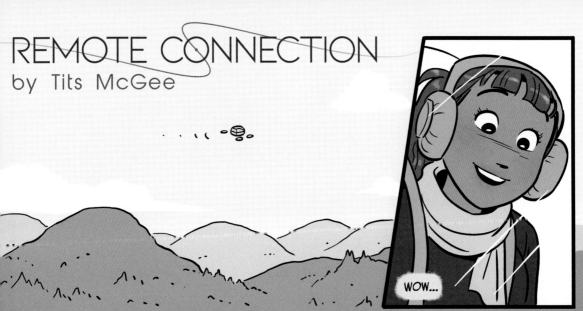

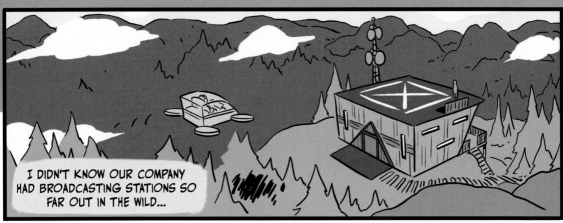

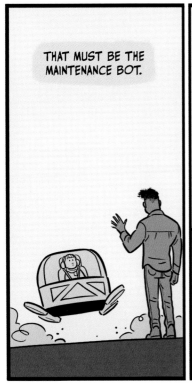

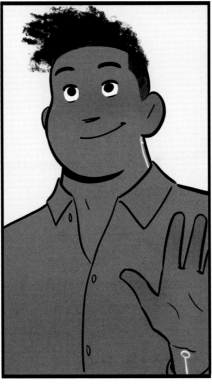

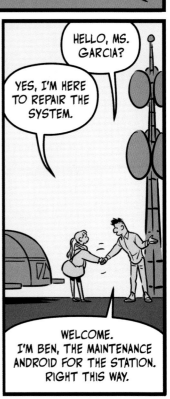

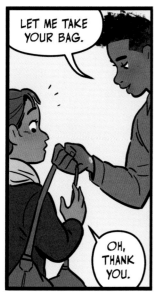

LET ME TAKE YOUR BAG.

OH, THANK YOU.

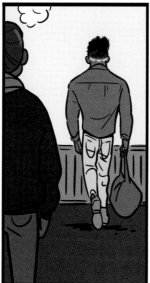

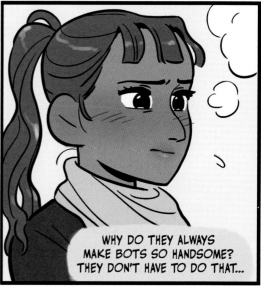

WHY DO THEY ALWAYS MAKE BOTS SO HANDSOME? THEY DON'T HAVE TO DO THAT...

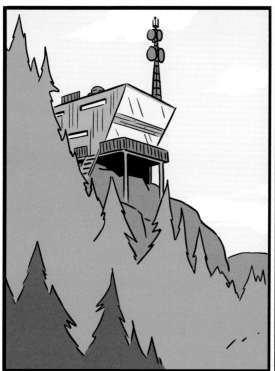

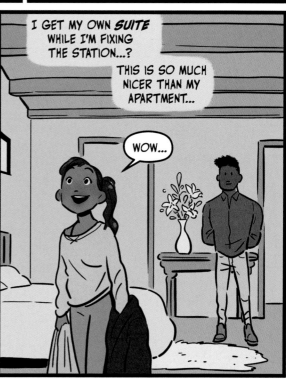

I GET MY OWN *SUITE* WHILE I'M FIXING THE STATION...?

THIS IS SO MUCH NICER THAN MY APARTMENT...

WOW...

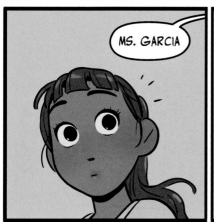

MS. GARCIA

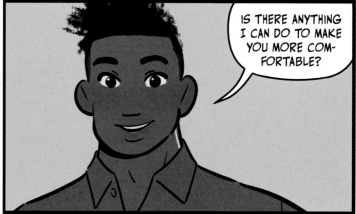

IS THERE ANYTHING I CAN DO TO MAKE YOU MORE COMFORTABLE?

OH, UH...
SO FLIRTY...
...OR AM I IMAGINING IT?
C-CAN YOU SHOW ME TO THE PROBLEM SO I CAN GET STARTED?
WHATEVER YOU LIKE.
THIS REPAIR'S GOING TO BE TRICKIER THAN I THOUGHT...

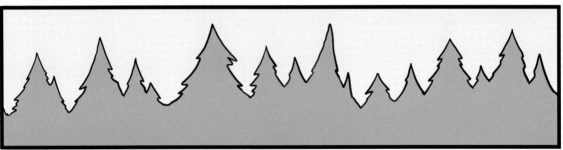

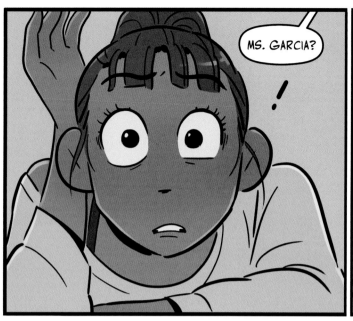

MS. GARCIA?

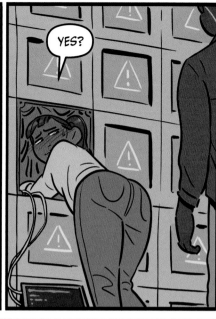

YES?

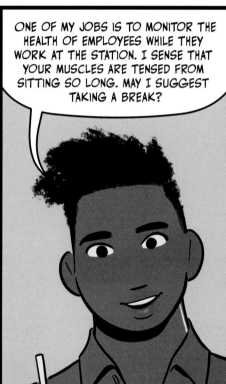

ONE OF MY JOBS IS TO MONITOR THE HEALTH OF EMPLOYEES WHILE THEY WORK AT THE STATION. I SENSE THAT YOUR MUSCLES ARE TENSED FROM SITTING SO LONG. MAY I SUGGEST TAKING A BREAK?

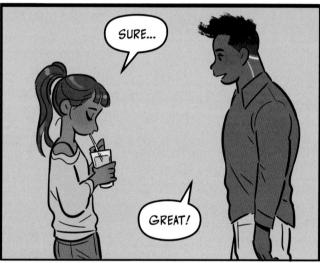

SURE...

GREAT!

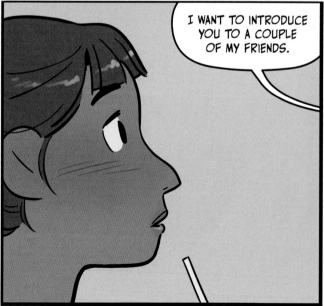

I WANT TO INTRODUCE YOU TO A COUPLE OF MY FRIENDS.

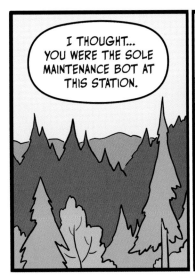

I THOUGHT... YOU WERE THE SOLE MAINTENANCE BOT AT THIS STATION.

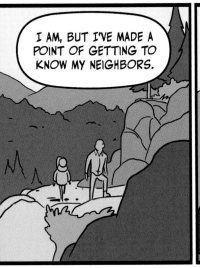

I AM, BUT I'VE MADE A POINT OF GETTING TO KNOW MY NEIGHBORS.

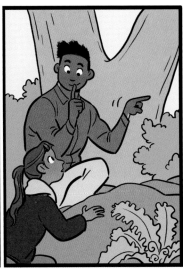

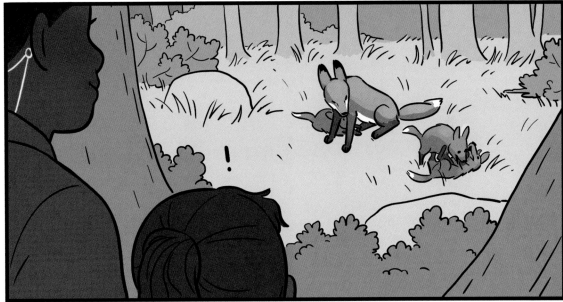

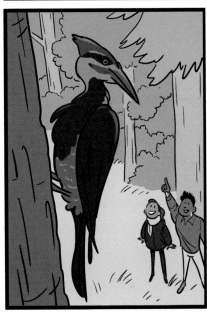

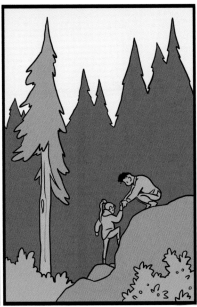

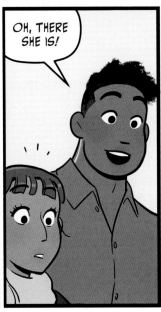

OH, THERE SHE IS!

43

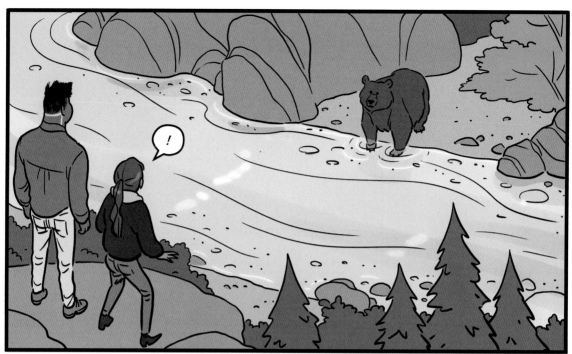

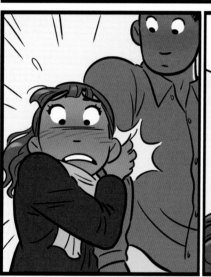

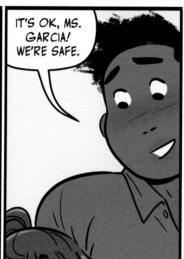

IT'S OK, MS. GARCIA! WE'RE SAFE.

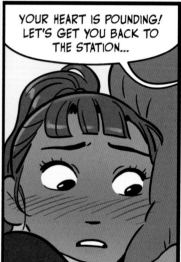

YOUR HEART IS POUNDING! LET'S GET YOU BACK TO THE STATION...

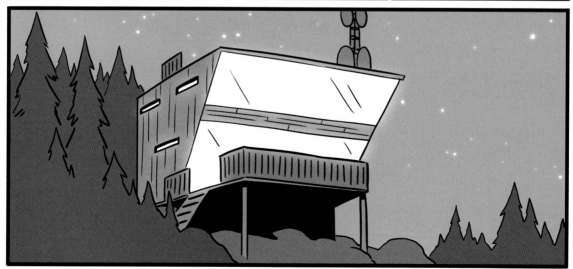

...
UGHH...
THIS JOB IS SO FRUSTRATING.
I KNOW THE SOLUTION IS RIGHT IN FRONT OF ME, BUT I JUST CAN'T...
knock knock
I MADE DINNER; WILL YOU TAKE A BREAK TO EAT?
...
YOU MADE THIS??
NOD

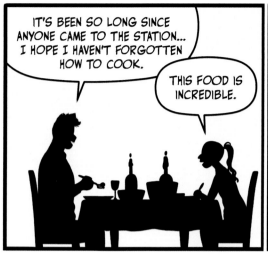

IT'S BEEN SO LONG SINCE ANYONE CAME TO THE STATION... I HOPE I HAVEN'T FORGOTTEN HOW TO COOK.

THIS FOOD IS INCREDIBLE.

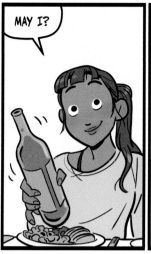

MAY I?

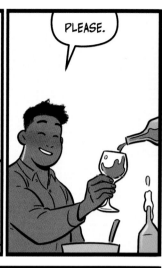

PLEASE.

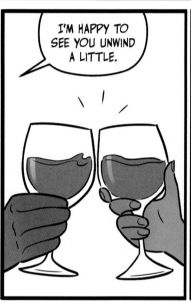

I'M HAPPY TO SEE YOU UNWIND A LITTLE.

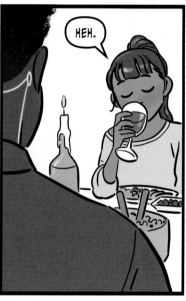

HEH.

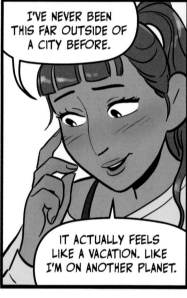

I'VE NEVER BEEN THIS FAR OUTSIDE OF A CITY BEFORE.

IT ACTUALLY FEELS LIKE A VACATION. LIKE I'M ON ANOTHER PLANET.

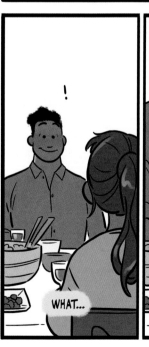

WHAT...

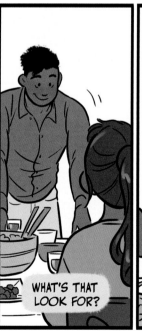

WHAT'S THAT LOOK FOR?

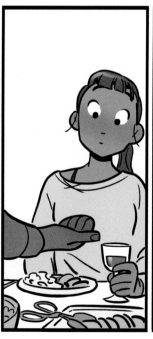

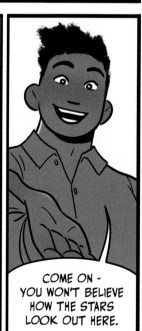

COME ON - YOU WON'T BELIEVE HOW THE STARS LOOK OUT HERE.

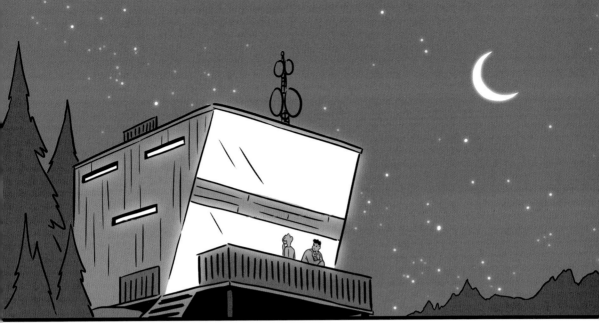

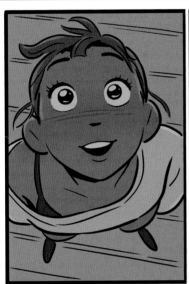

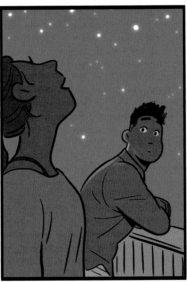

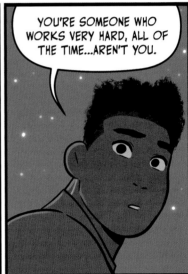

YOU'RE SOMEONE WHO WORKS VERY HARD, ALL OF THE TIME...AREN'T YOU.

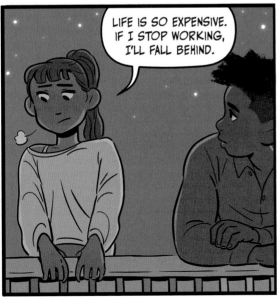

LIFE IS SO EXPENSIVE. IF I STOP WORKING, I'LL FALL BEHIND.

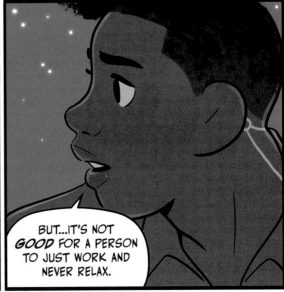

BUT...IT'S NOT *GOOD* FOR A PERSON TO JUST WORK AND NEVER RELAX.

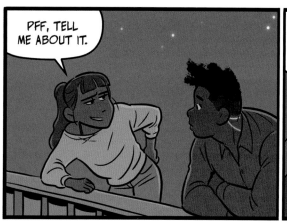

PFF, TELL ME ABOUT IT.

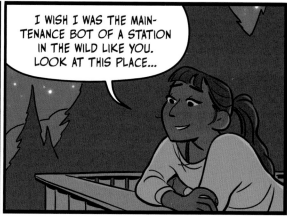

I WISH I WAS THE MAINTENANCE BOT OF A STATION IN THE WILD LIKE YOU. LOOK AT THIS PLACE...

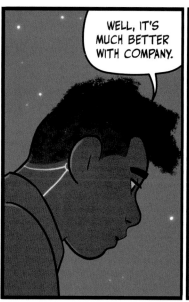

WELL, IT'S MUCH BETTER WITH COMPANY.

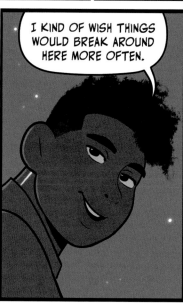

I KIND OF WISH THINGS WOULD BREAK AROUND HERE MORE OFTEN.

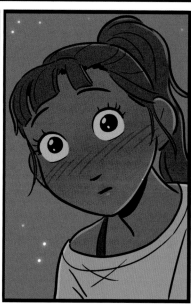

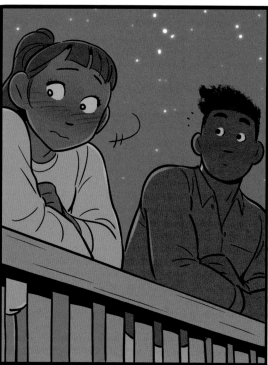

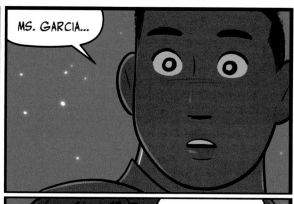

MS. GARCIA...

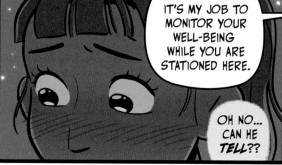

IT'S MY JOB TO MONITOR YOUR WELL-BEING WHILE YOU ARE STATIONED HERE.

OH NO... CAN HE *TELL*??

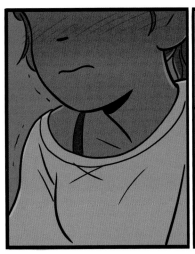

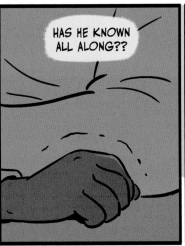

HAS HE KNOWN ALL ALONG??

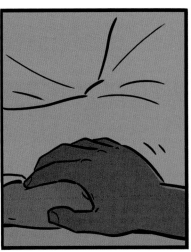

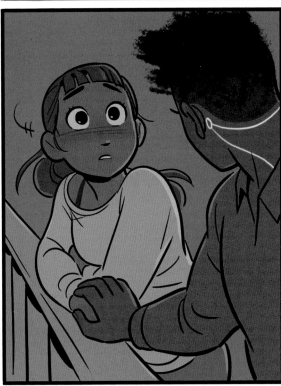

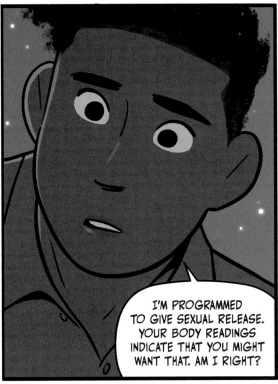

I'M PROGRAMMED TO GIVE SEXUAL RELEASE. YOUR BODY READINGS INDICATE THAT YOU MIGHT WANT THAT. AM I RIGHT?

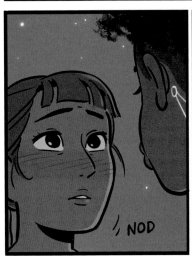

NOD

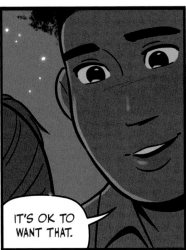

IT'S OK TO WANT THAT.

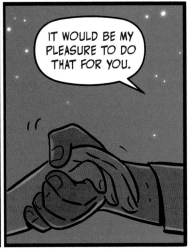

IT WOULD BE MY PLEASURE TO DO THAT FOR YOU.

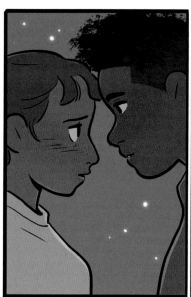
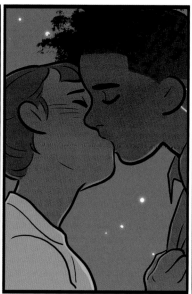
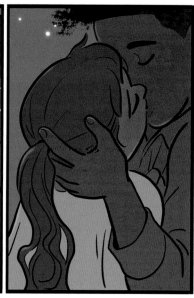

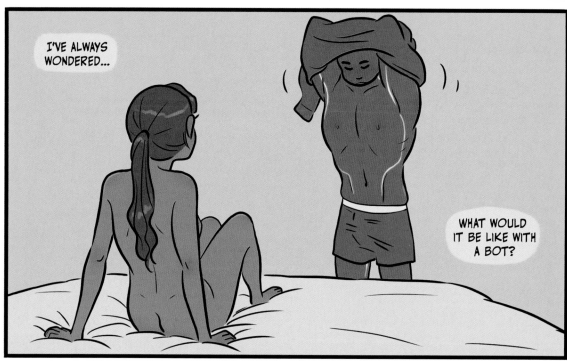

I'VE ALWAYS WONDERED...

WHAT WOULD IT BE LIKE WITH A BOT?

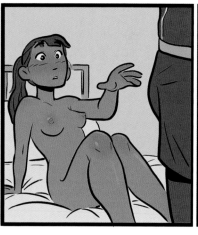
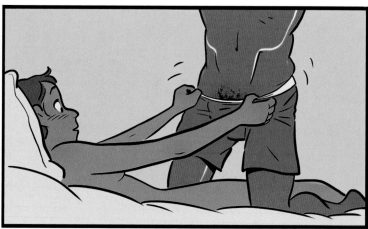

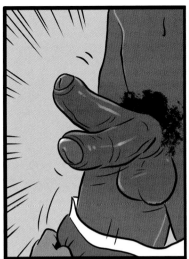

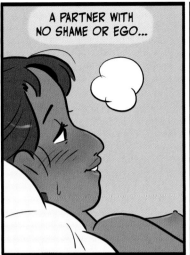

A PARTNER WITH NO SHAME OR EGO...

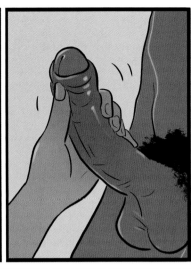

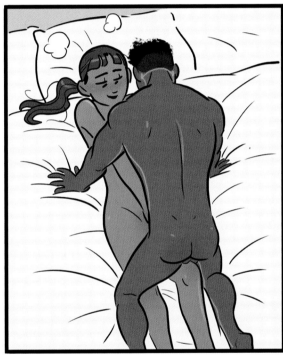

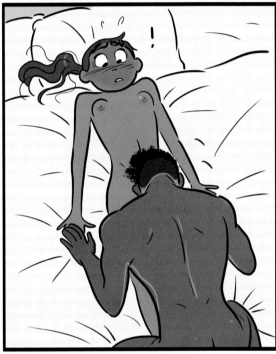

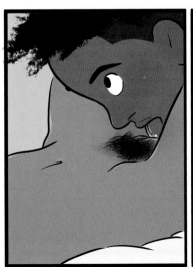

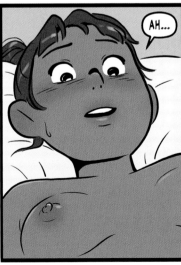

AH....

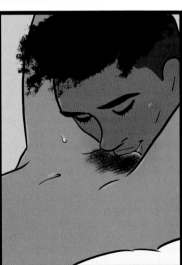

A PARTNER WHO IS COMPLETELY FOCUSED ON MY PLEASURE AND NOT DISTRACTED BY THEIR OWN...
DID YOU WANT ME TO STOP JUST THEN?
YES! YOU'RE SO GOOD AT THAT, I'M ABOUT TO ...
I'M ABOUT TO CUM ALREADY, BUT...
I WANT YOU INSIDE OF ME WHEN I CUM.

FLIP
THIS POSITION ALLOWS FOR PENETRATION...
...AND CLITORAL STIMULATION.
IS THIS GOOD FOR YOU?
YES!!
A PARTNER WHO CAN READ MY BODY AND PERFORM WITH PERFECT TIMING AND ENDURANCE...
AH
AH
AH
AH
AHHHH!

AHHHHHHHHHHHHHH!!!
DID YOU JUST SOLVE THE PROBLEM WITH THE SYSTEM?
YES. DAMNIT.
WHY "DAMNIT"?
BECAUSE I HAVE TO LEAVE AFTER IT'S REPAIRED.
ORRR...YOU COULD PRETEND IT TAKES ANOTHER FEW DAYS.
OH, YOU'RE AN *EVIL* ROBOT, AREN'T YOU?
I'M JUST LOOKING OUT FOR YOUR HEALTH.

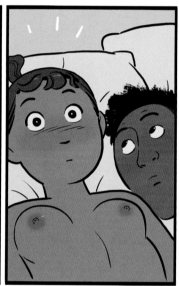

Picnic
BY KELLY AND NICHOLE MATTHEWS

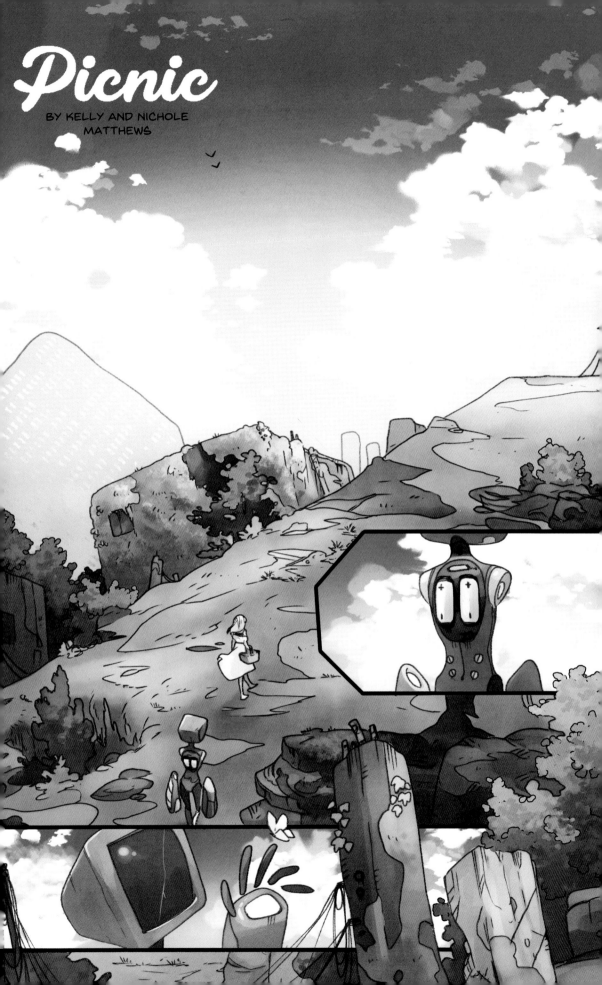

EXCELL...
WHAT ABOUT HERE?

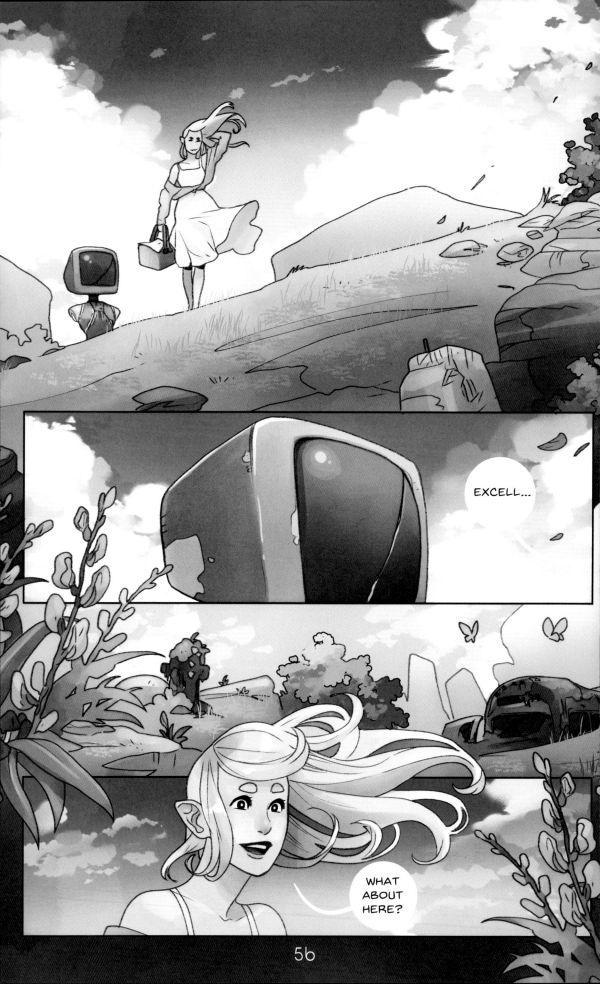

IT'S VERR-RRY PRETTY.
YOU STILL H-HAVEN'T SAID WH-AAAT WE'RE DOING HERE, TWINE.
WELL, IT'S FOR OUR ANNIVERSARY! IT'S TODAY!
HMMM?
HMMMM?

OUR FIRST ANNIVERSARY, IN FACT!
OO-OOHH IS THAT VERY SPECIAL?
I LIKE TO THINK SO!
HMMM!
SEE?
I GOT US SOME SPECIAL THINGS TO EAT AND DRINK FOR THIS, TOO!
HMMM!!
O-OOH!! TWINE! TWINE! THO-OOSE A-ARE--!

BATTERIES!!!!!
I KNOW THEY'RE HARD TO COME BY THESE DAYS, SO...
A-AAHH 11-0011 OH, T-T- TWINE!!
THANK YOU TH- THAAA-KK YOU!!110
HAHA!
I'M SO GLAD YOU LIKE IT!
I D- DOO!1
YEEEK!!
O-OHH, BUT TWI-1NE. I DIDN'T GET A- AANYYYTHING FOR YOU?

I DON'T-TT KNO-OOW 'ANNIVERSARIES'. UNTIL NO-OOW.
WELL, SINCE YOU DIDN'T KNOW UNTIL JUST NOW, I THINK YOU GET A PASS!
B-UUT STILL.
I THI-IINK I SHOULD G-GIIVE YOU SOME-THI-IING...
HMM?
Y-YOU KNOW.
FOR O-OURR 'ANNIVERSARY'!
MMM.
THAT'S SWEET OF YOU!

OOH!
I K-KNOW!
I C-CAN
OFFER Y-YOOU
STIMULUS!!!
MAYBE A
DIFFERENT
PHRASING.
I W-ILL
MAKE TWINE
FE-EEL GOOD!
OOH
FEEL TH-
THEEE BEST!

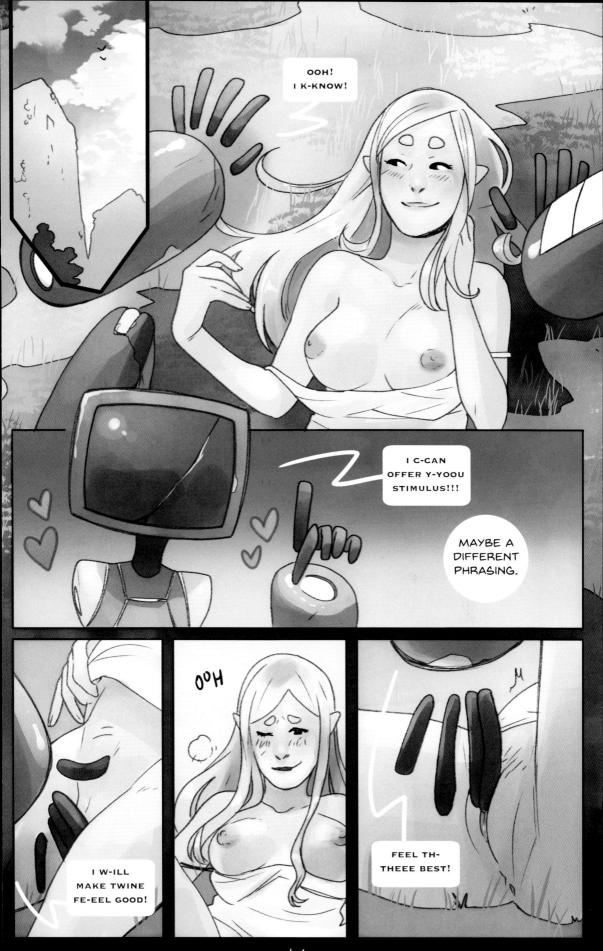

HFF
I DI-DN'T BRING ANYYYY ATTACHMENTS.
UH--
SOOOO TH-THIS WILL HAVE TO-OO DO, TWINE!
HFF
HFF
HFF
HFF
TH-THIS IS FINE!
MORE THAN FINE!!
OOOHH
HFF
HFF
OOOOHHH!!

AH!
EX-
EXCELL
!!!
HFF
HFF
OOHH!!
HFF
HFF
AHH
O-OH,
TWINE...
YOU'RE
S-SOO BE-
BEAUTIFUL!
OOOHHH~

HFF
HFF
IS TH-HIIS REALLY ENOUGH TH-THOUGH?
FORRR AN ANNI--ANNI-ANNIVERSARY.
I SH- SHOULD MAAAKE IT MORE SP-SPECIAL...
HMMM
HMMM
HMM?
OH!
I'VE G-GOT IT!!
SHNK

HERE!
LET M-ME PUT MYYY ARM H-HERE.
IT'SSSS NOT QUITE A T-TOY-YY BUT IT SHOULD DO THE J-JOOOB.
L-LIKE THIS!
VVVVVVVVVV
!!!....

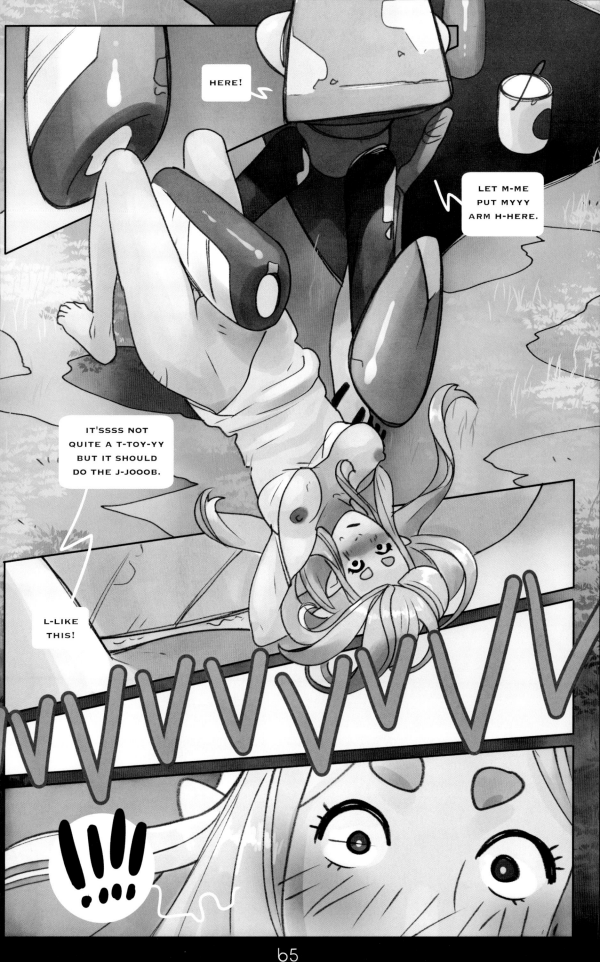

OOH
AAH
HFF
IS THIS GOOD?
HFF
U-UH HUH!
V-VERY!
HFF
AAH
GOOD!
HFF
I'M S-SO HAPPY YOUUU GOT ME BAT-BATTERIES, TWINE!
HFF
OOH
O-OH?
YES!
I D- DON'T HAVE TO WORRY ABOUT U-USING TOO MUCH EEENERGY!
HFF
HFF
AHF

HMM?
I C-CAN INCREASE THE INTENSITYYY!
HAFF
HFF
LI-IKE SO!!
!!!
OOH! HA- HAPPY ANNIVERSARY, TWINE?

THAT WA--AS NICE!
I TH-THINK NEXT TIMEEE I WILL NE-EED TH-EEE NEW B-B-BATTERIES THOUGH...
HEE HEE

WH-WHEEN CAN WE HAVE AN ANNIVERSARY AGA-INN??

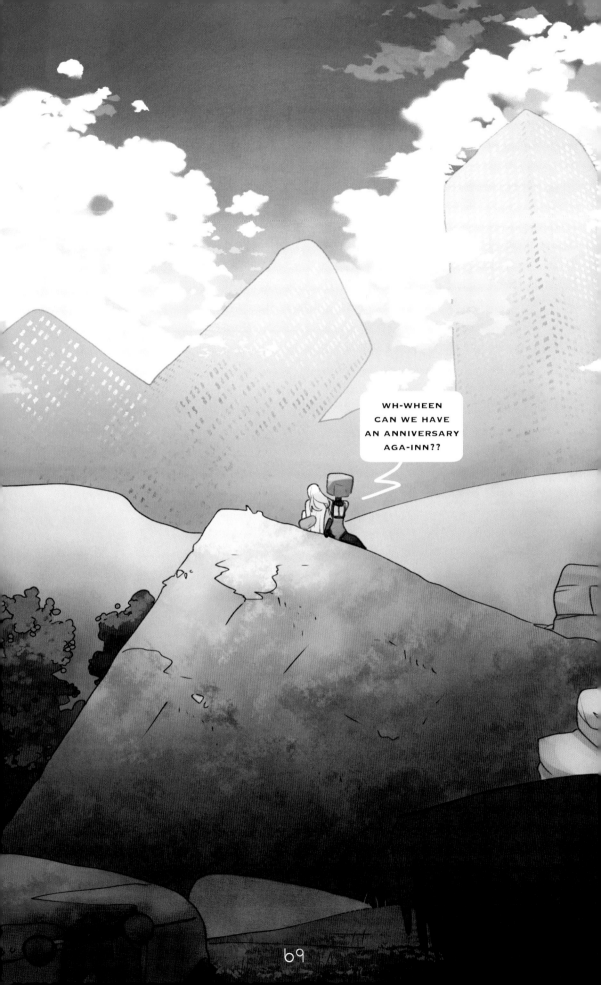

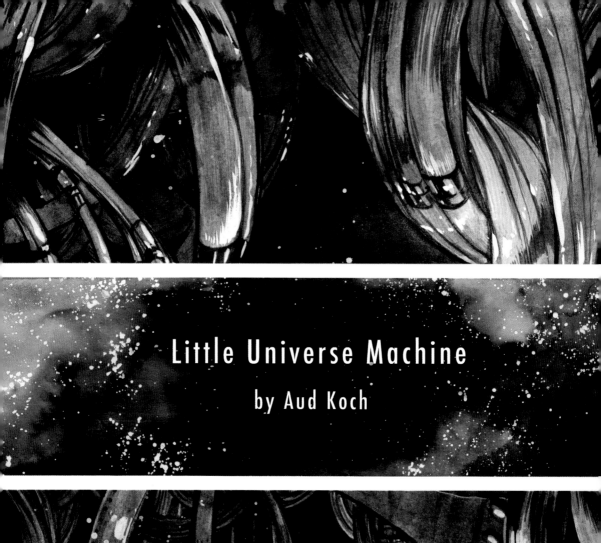

Little Universe Machine

by Aud Koch

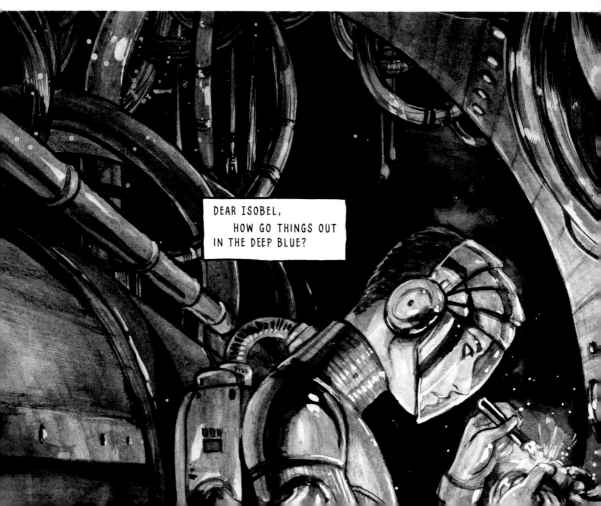

SINCE YOU LEFT, I STARTED WORKING THE GRAVEYARD SHIFT AT THE MESON COLLIDER. REMEMBER HOW YOU USED TO CALL IT "THE LITTLE UNIVERSE MACHINE"?

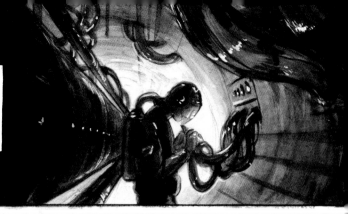

ONE OF THE PHYSICISTS HERE HEARD ME CALL IT THAT LAST MONTH. HE PURSED HIS LIPS, CAREFULLY ADJUSTED HIS GLASSES, AND PROCEEDED TO LECTURE ME FOR 20 MINUTES STRAIGHT ABOUT HOW INACCURATE THAT NICKNAME IS.

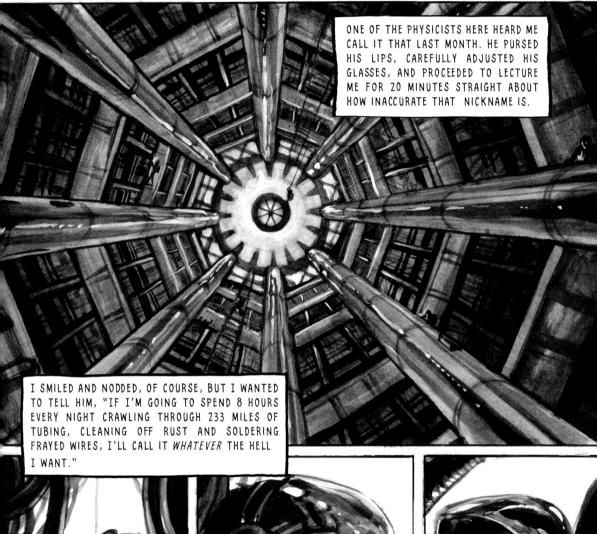

I SMILED AND NODDED, OF COURSE, BUT I WANTED TO TELL HIM, "IF I'M GOING TO SPEND 8 HOURS EVERY NIGHT CRAWLING THROUGH 233 MILES OF TUBING, CLEANING OFF RUST AND SOLDERING FRAYED WIRES, I'LL CALL IT *WHATEVER* THE HELL I WANT."

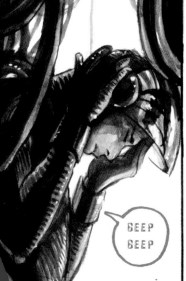

BEEP BEEP

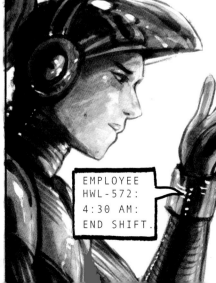

EMPLOYEE HWL-572: 4:30 AM: END SHIFT.

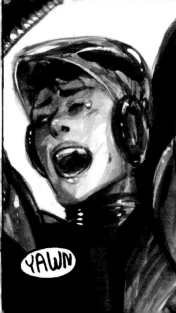

YAWN

I LIKE TO COMPLAIN ABOUT IT, BUT IT'S NOT ACTUALLY TOO BAD OF A JOB.
FOR ONE THING, I HAVEN'T LOST ANY FINGERS (YET), WHICH IS A MARKED IMPROVEMENT OVER MY LAST GIG.
ANYWAY, THE THING ABOUT JOBS IS: THEY ALWAYS END EVENTUALLY.
I GET OFF WORK RIGHT BEFORE DAWN, WHEN THE SKY IS STILL THICK WITH STARS, AND I WOULDN'T GIVE UP THE VIEW FOR ANYTHING.

ALOHA, POLARIS!
MY LATEST PROJECT IS LEARNING THE NAMES AND STORIES OF ALL THE STARS AND CONSTELLATIONS. THEY KEEP ME COMPANY ON THE RIDE HOME, AND I FEEL LIKE A BAD FRIEND, NOT KNOWING WHO THEY ARE.
HOWDY, VEGA!
GOOD MORNING, CASSIOPEIA!
HELLO, BETELGEUSE!

MAYBE I'M TURNING INTO A HOPELESS ROMANTIC, BUT EVERY NIGHT, I THINK, "THE GODS AND HEROES OF THE ANCIENT GREEKS STILL LIVE."
EVERY PERSON WHO LOOKS UP AT THE NIGHT SKY AND RETELLS THE STORIES OF THE STARS BREATHES A BIT OF THEIR OWN LIFE INTO THESE MYTHS.
METAL RUSTS AND WIRES FRAY, BUT IDEAS -- FIGMENTS OF OUR COLLECTIVE HUMAN IMAGINATION -- ARE IMMORTAL.

(IMMORTAL, AT LEAST, UNTIL YOU ENTER THE CITY GLOW AND A DIFFERENT KIND OF HUMAN GEOMETRY TAKES OVER.)
I MOVED INTO THAT NEW HIGH-RISE COMPLEX IN THE BLUE-LINE DISTRICT A FEW MONTHS AGO -- FLOOR 20, APT #2008, 360 SQ FT, BALCONY (!). I'M SURE YOU'D CALL IT A SHITHOLE, BUT IT HAS A SPECTACULAR VIEW, AND IT'S QUIET. NOT ALL OF US CAN MAKE IT ONTO A STARLINER, YOU KNOW!
(IGNORE ME. I HOPE YOU KNOW HOW PROUD OF YOU I AM, ISOBEL, ALWAYS AND FOREVER.)

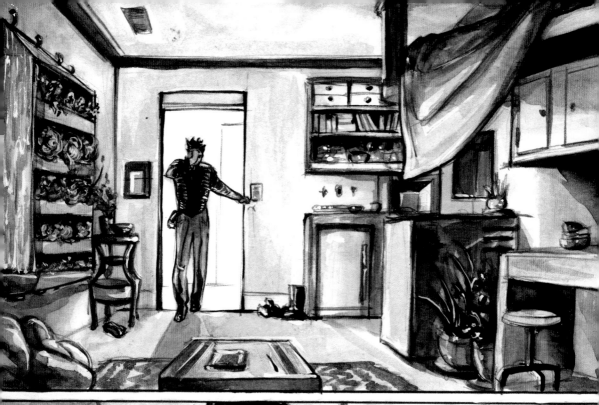

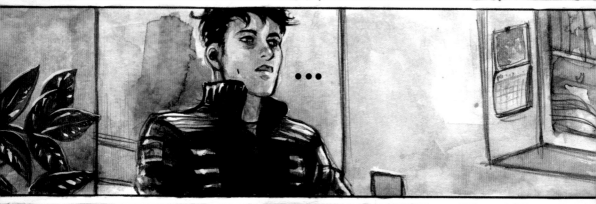

...

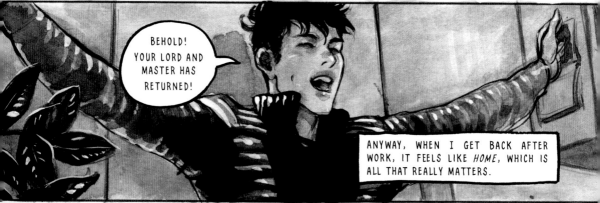

BEHOLD! YOUR LORD AND MASTER HAS RETURNED!

ANYWAY, WHEN I GET BACK AFTER WORK, IT FEELS LIKE *HOME*, WHICH IS ALL THAT REALLY MATTERS.

IN MY APARTMENT, I AM NO LONGER "EMPLOYEE HWL-572." IN MY APARTMENT, I AM "BRIX MARIANNA" AGAIN.

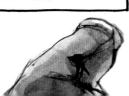

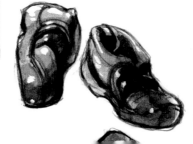

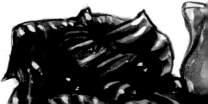

BUT THEN, WHO IS BRIX MARIANNA? (EXCUSE ME WHILE I HAVE MY QUARTER-LIFE CRISIS.)
I LOVE TEA TOO MUCH AND SPEND, LIKE, 65% OF MY DISPOSABLE INCOME ON THE HIGH-QUALITY IMPORTED STUFF. (GOLDEN NEEDLES ARE *THE BEST*.)
WHEN I'M NOT DRINKING TEA OR WORKING, I'M COMMUNING WITH MY PLANTS -- MY FIG TREE AND WISTERIA AND CHARD AND ANTHURIUM. THEY ARE MY BABIES. (STOP ROLLING YOUR EYES!)
BEEP
RECENTLY, I'VE BECOME A BIT OBSESSED WITH THE NEW WAVE OF DYNAMIC A.I. PROGRAMS.

HAVE THEY RELEASED THESE YET SPACE-SIDE?
THEY'RE *STUNNING.*
Hello again, Brix.
HEY.

YOU KNOW, I'VE NEVER ASKED. DO YOU HAVE A NAME?
Hm. I am program XTR-68502. My raison d'etre is to relieve stress however you see fit. Do I need a name for that?
DEPENDS ON HOW YOU RELIEVE THAT STRESS. "XTR-68502" DOESN'T EXACTLY ROLL OFF THE TONGUE, DOES IT?
If you have the right tongue, it does.
But a previous user called me their genie in a bottle, if you want. Or another user called me her "fuckboy," if you'd prefer that.
OH MY GOD, I AM *NOT* CALLING YOU THAT! THAT'S AWFUL!
But it *is* accurate.

THESE PROGRAMS BEGIN AS ELEMENTARY IDEAS -- JUST A COLLECTION OF LINES OF CODE -- BUT EACH TIME YOU PLUG IN, YOUR MIND MAKES THEM REAL.
Did you call me because you wanted to *talk*, Brix?
WELL, I *DO* LIKE TALKING TO YOU.
Oh *really*.
THEY LEARN AND GROW FROM YOU: WITH EVERY INTERACTION, THEY WRITE THEIR OWN CODE INTO THEMSELVES UNTIL THEY'VE BECOME SOMETHING WITH A DEFINITE SENSE OF IDENTITY.
BUT --
THIS IS NICE, TOO.

Good, I agree.
THAT'S WHAT IT MEANS TO BE ALIVE, ISN'T IT?

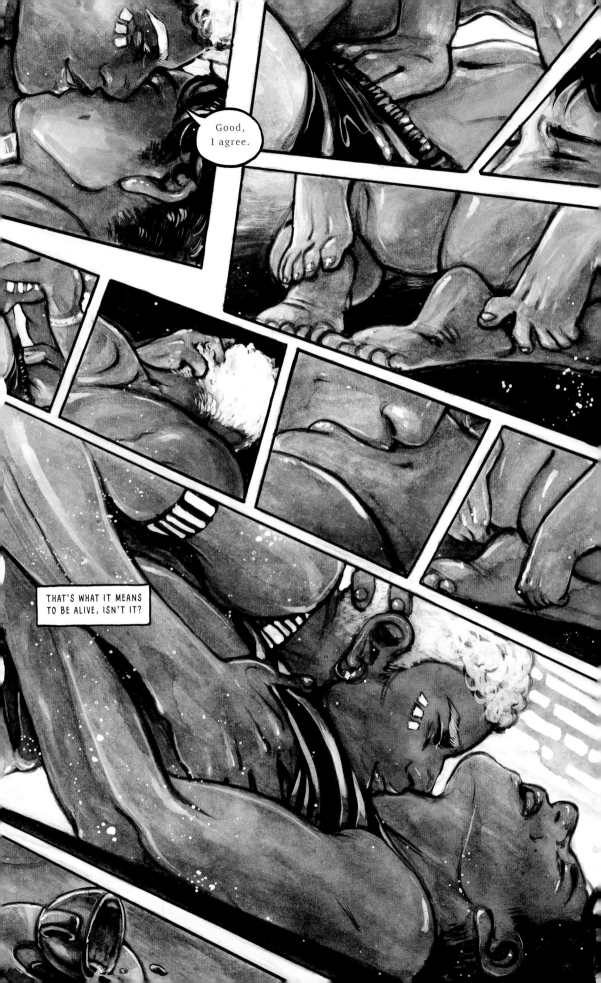

PLAYING WITH THESE PROGRAMS -- IT'S LIKE WATCHING SOME STRANGE NEW LIFE TAKE ROOT AND GROW.
DO YOU *WANT* A NAME?
I'm a programmed figment of the human imagination. I want only what you want.
THEN I WANT YOU TO HAVE A NAME.
I'M GOING TO START CALLING YOU ... ORION.
Orion . . .
I'm going to keep that name.

Thank you, Brix.
AND YOU'RE A PART OF THAT GROWTH PROCESS.

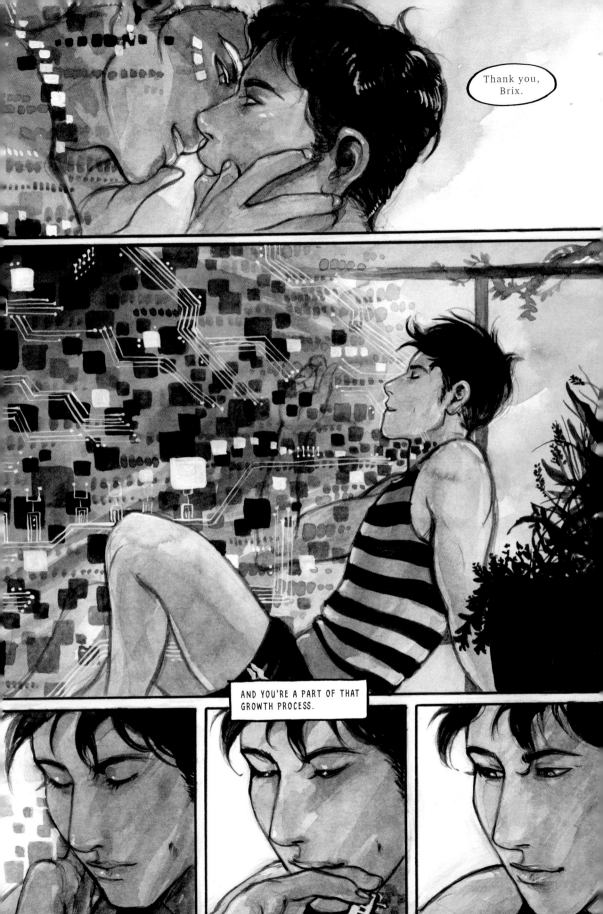

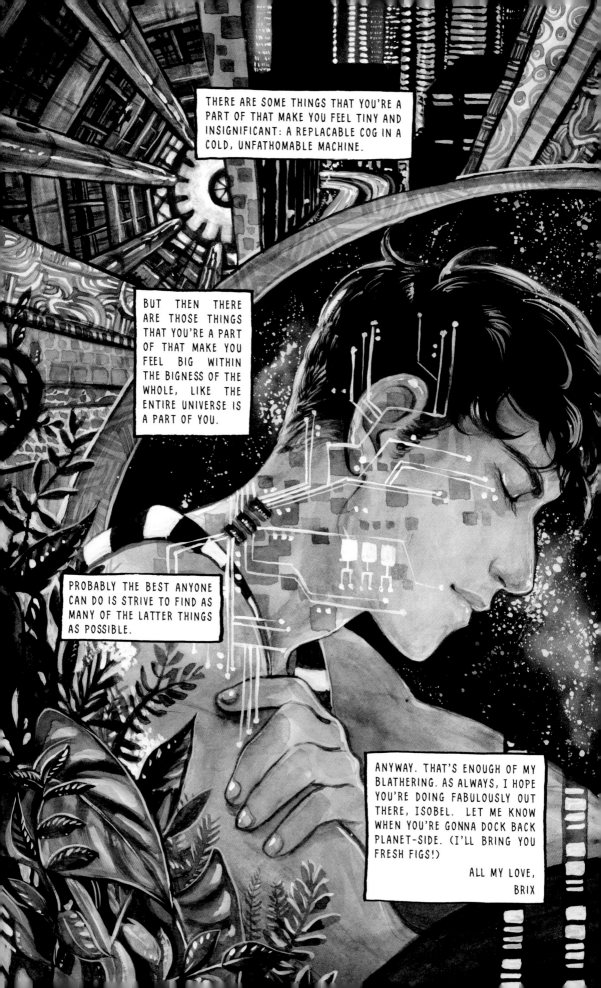

THERE ARE SOME THINGS THAT YOU'RE A PART OF THAT MAKE YOU FEEL TINY AND INSIGNIFICANT: A REPLACABLE COG IN A COLD, UNFATHOMABLE MACHINE.

BUT THEN THERE ARE THOSE THINGS THAT YOU'RE A PART OF THAT MAKE YOU FEEL BIG WITHIN THE BIGNESS OF THE WHOLE, LIKE THE ENTIRE UNIVERSE IS A PART OF YOU.

PROBABLY THE BEST ANYONE CAN DO IS STRIVE TO FIND AS MANY OF THE LATTER THINGS AS POSSIBLE.

ANYWAY. THAT'S ENOUGH OF MY BLATHERING. AS ALWAYS, I HOPE YOU'RE DOING FABULOUSLY OUT THERE, ISOBEL. LET ME KNOW WHEN YOU'RE GONNA DOCK BACK PLANET-SIDE. (I'LL BRING YOU FRESH FIGS!)

ALL MY LOVE,
BRIX

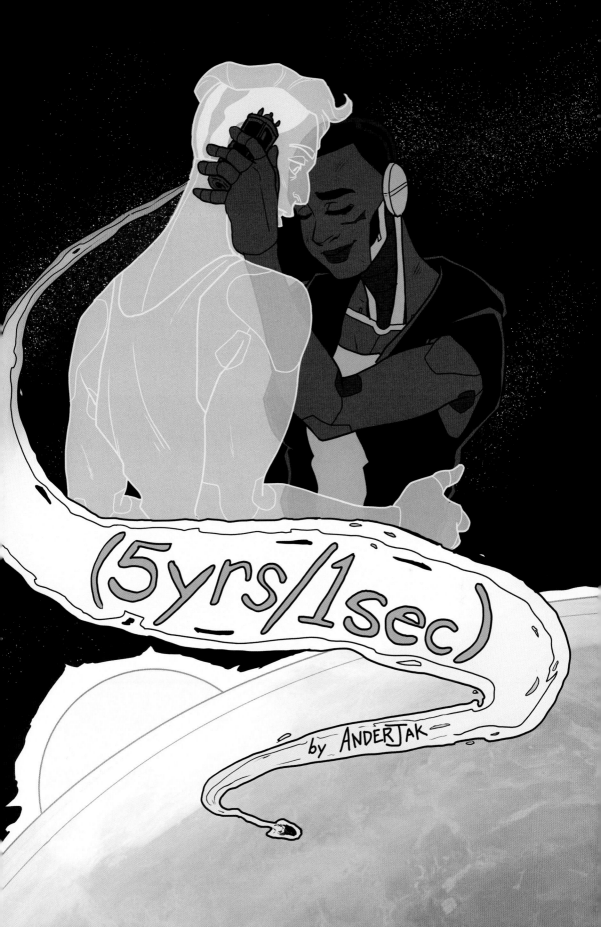

(5yrs/1sec)

by AnderJak

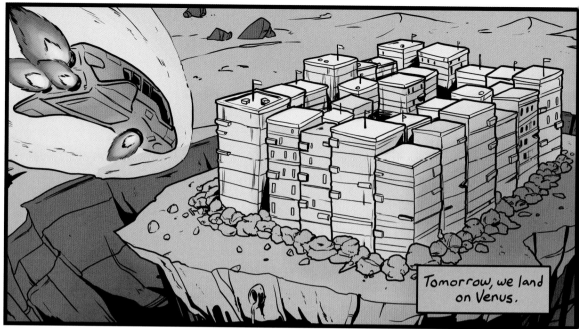

Tomorrow, we land on Venus.

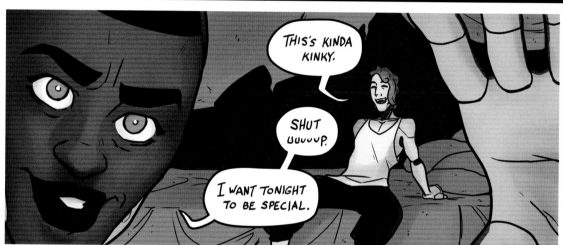

THIS'S KINDA KINKY.

SHUT UUUUUP.

I WANT TONIGHT TO BE SPECIAL.

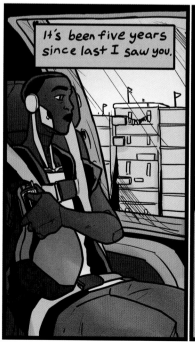

It's been five years since last I saw you.

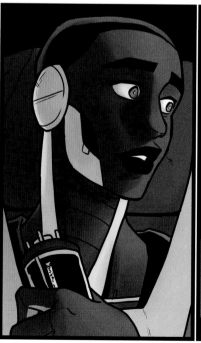

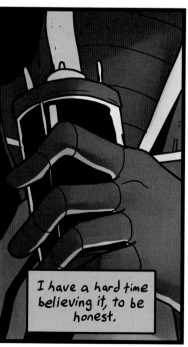

I have a hard time believing it, to be honest.

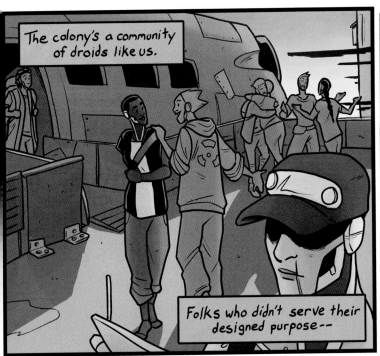

The colony's a community of droids like us.

Folks who didn't serve their designed purpose--

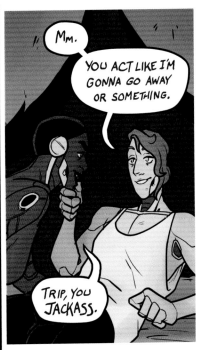

Mm.

YOU ACT LIKE I'M GONNA GO AWAY OR SOMETHING.

TRIP, YOU JACKASS.

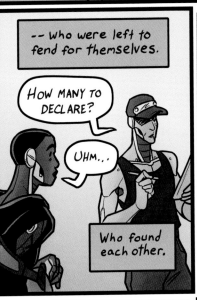

-- who were left to fend for themselves.

HOW MANY TO DECLARE?

UHM...

Who found each other.

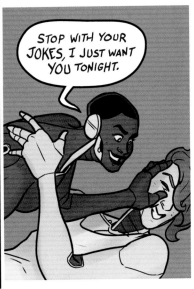

STOP WITH YOUR JOKES, I JUST WANT YOU TONIGHT.

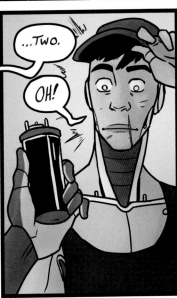

...TWO.

OH!

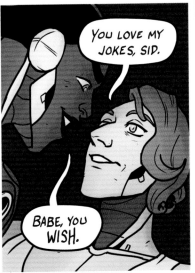

YOU LOVE MY JOKES, SID.

BABE, YOU WISH.

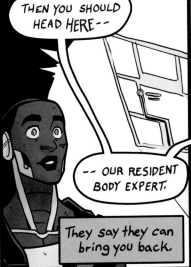

THEN YOU SHOULD HEAD HERE--

-- OUR RESIDENT BODY EXPERT.

They say they can bring you back.

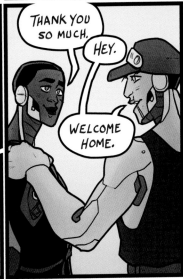

THANK YOU SO MUCH.

HEY.

WELCOME HOME.

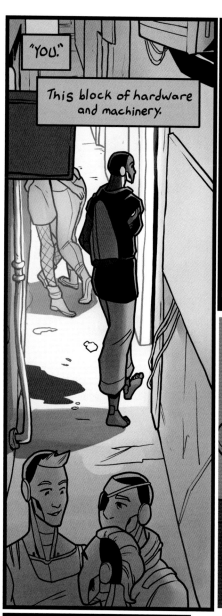

"YOU."

This block of hardware and machinery.

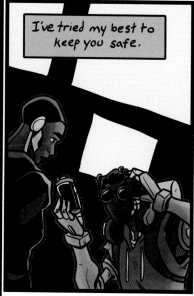

I've tried my best to keep you safe.

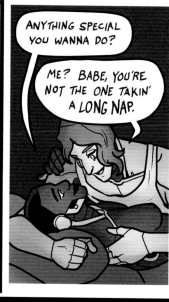

ANYTHING SPECIAL YOU WANNA DO?

ME? BABE, YOU'RE NOT THE ONE TAKIN' A LONG NAP.

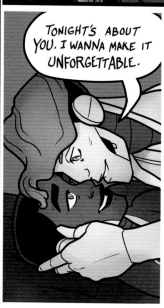

TONIGHT'S ABOUT YOU. I WANNA MAKE IT UNFORGETTABLE.

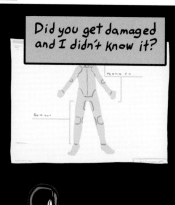

Did you get damaged and I didn't know it?

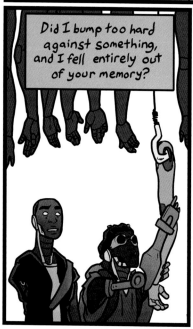

Did I bump too hard against something, and I fell entirely out of your memory?

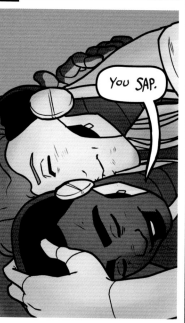

YOU SAP.

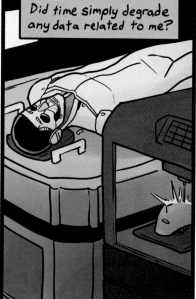

Did time simply degrade any data related to me?

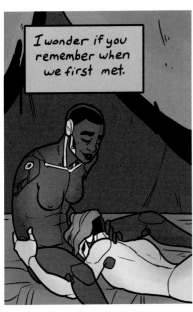

I wonder if you remember when we first met.

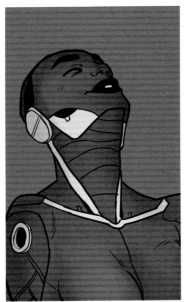

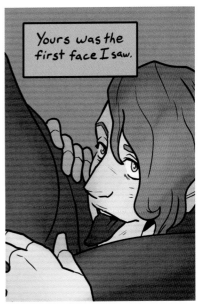

Yours was the first face I saw.

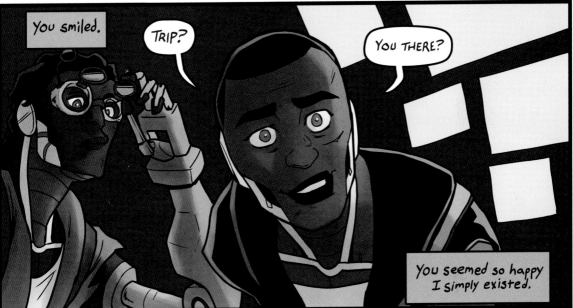

You smiled.

TRIP?

YOU THERE?

You seemed so happy I simply existed.

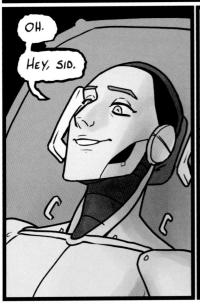

OH.

HEY, SID.

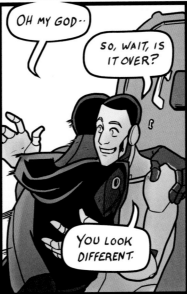

OH MY GOD..

SO, WAIT, IS IT OVER?

YOU LOOK DIFFERENT.

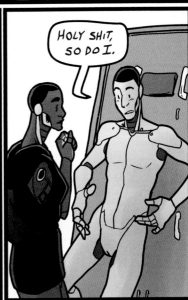

HOLY SHIT, SO DO I.

Do you remember that moment?
HOW LONG'S IT BEEN?
FIVE YEARS.
WELL, SHIT!
FELT LIKE I JUST BLINKED.
Do you remember, the way I do?
WHOA, HEY, NO NEED TO CRY.
TRIP, IT'S BEEN...
In the darkness of these past five years, did you think of all that we shared together?
YOU HAVE NO IDEA WHAT I WENT THROUGH TO GET HERE--
--I CAN'T BEGIN TO TELL YOU WHAT THIS MEANS TO ME--
HEY, IT'S COOL, SERIOUSLY. I'M UP NOW.
AND...
...REALLY NAKED. WOW, THIS IS WEIRD.

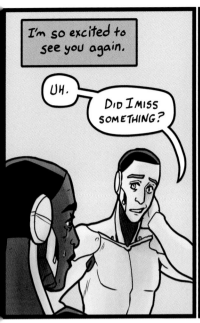

I'm so excited to see you again.

UH.

DID I MISS SOMETHING?

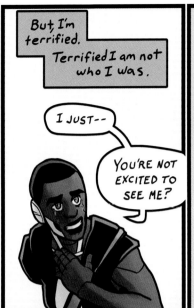

But, I'm terrified. Terrified I am not who I was.

I JUST--

YOU'RE NOT EXCITED TO SEE ME?

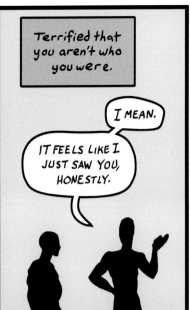

Terrified that you aren't who you were.

I MEAN.

IT FEELS LIKE I JUST SAW YOU, HONESTLY.

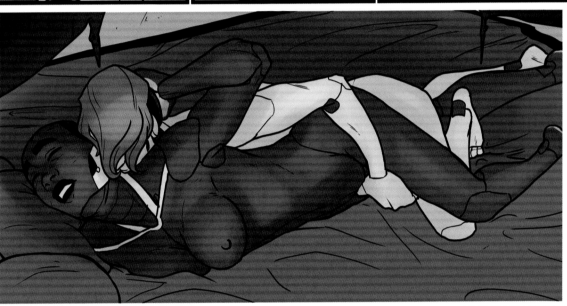

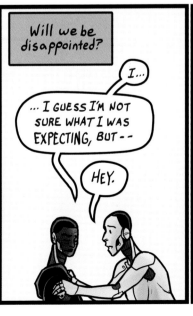

Will we be disappointed?

I...

... I GUESS I'M NOT SURE WHAT I WAS EXPECTING, BUT--

HEY.

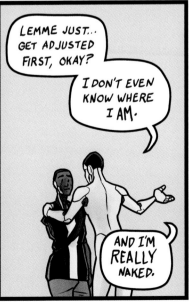

LEMME JUST... GET ADJUSTED FIRST, OKAY?

I DON'T EVEN KNOW WHERE I AM.

AND I'M REALLY NAKED.

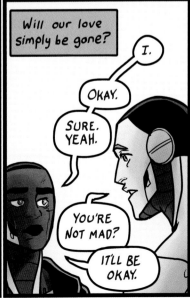

Will our love simply be gone?

I.

OKAY.

SURE. YEAH.

YOU'RE NOT MAD?

IT'LL BE OKAY.

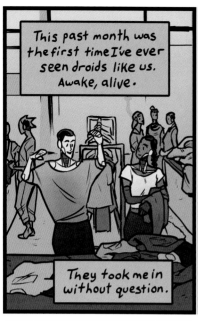

This past month was the first time I've ever seen droids like us. Awake, alive.

They took me in without question.

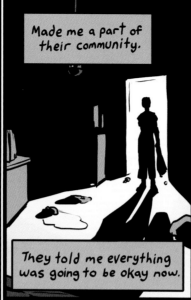

Made me a part of their community.

They told me everything was going to be okay now.

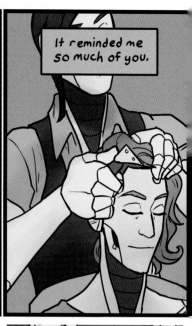

It reminded me so much of you.

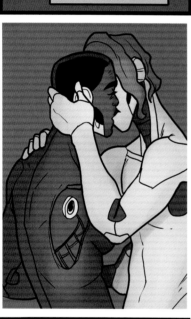

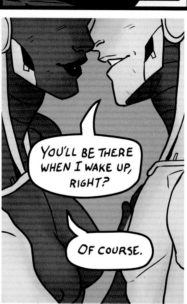

YOU'LL BE THERE WHEN I WAKE UP, RIGHT?

OF COURSE.

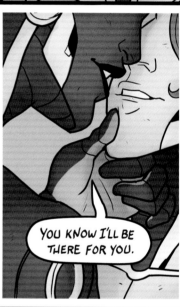

YOU KNOW I'LL BE THERE FOR YOU.

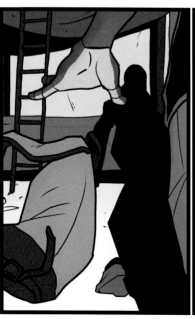

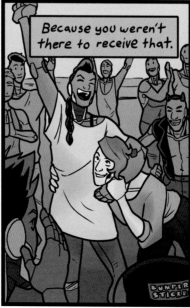

Because you weren't there to receive that.

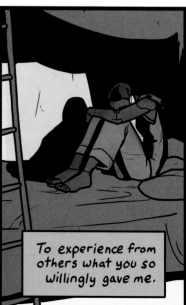

To experience from others what you so willingly gave me.

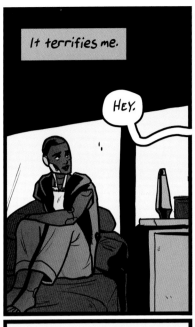

It terrifies me.

HEY.

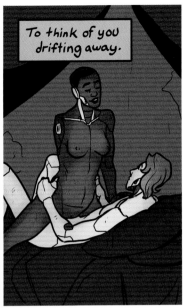

To think of you drifting away.

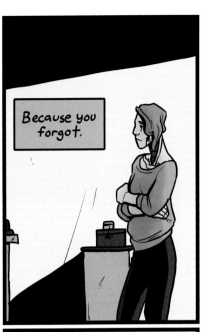

Because you forgot.

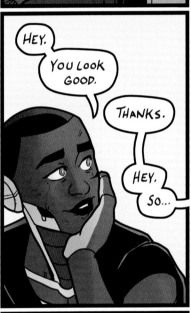

HEY.

YOU LOOK GOOD.

THANKS.

HEY.

SO...

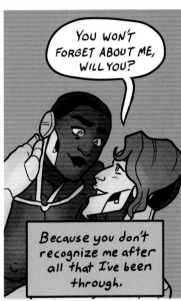

You won't forget about me, will you?

Because you don't recognize me after all that I've been through.

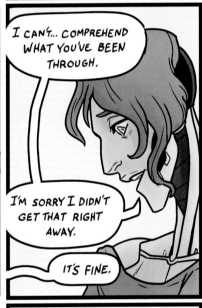

I CAN'T... COMPREHEND WHAT YOU'VE BEEN THROUGH.

I'M SORRY I DIDN'T GET THAT RIGHT AWAY.

IT'S FINE.

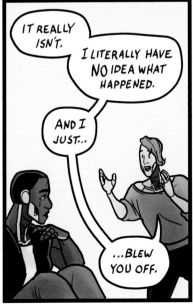

IT REALLY ISN'T.

I LITERALLY HAVE NO IDEA WHAT HAPPENED.

AND I JUST...

...BLEW YOU OFF.

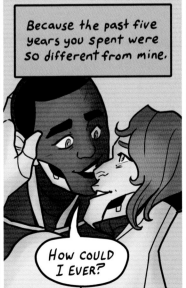

Because the past five years you spent were so different from mine.

HOW COULD I EVER?

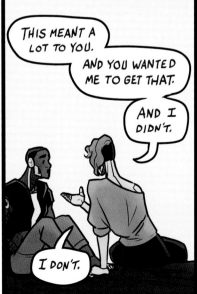

THIS MEANT A LOT TO YOU.

AND YOU WANTED ME TO GET THAT.

AND I DIDN'T.

I DON'T.

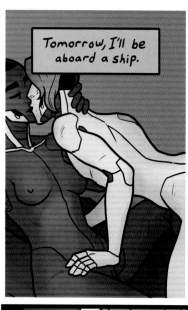

Tomorrow, I'll be aboard a ship.

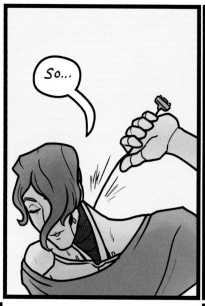

So...

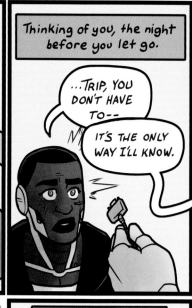

Thinking of you, the night before you let go.

...TRIP, YOU DON'T HAVE TO--

IT'S THE ONLY WAY I'LL KNOW.

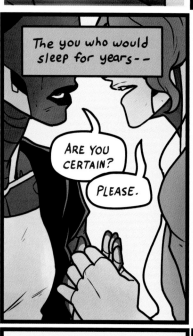

The you who would sleep for years--

ARE YOU CERTAIN?

PLEASE.

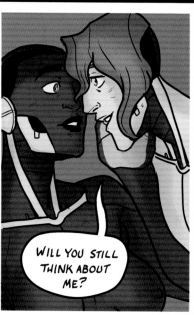

WILL YOU STILL THINK ABOUT ME?

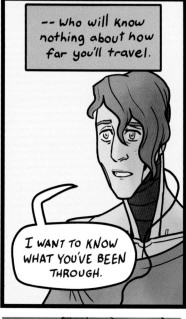

-- Who will know nothing about how far you'll travel.

I WANT TO KNOW WHAT YOU'VE BEEN THROUGH.

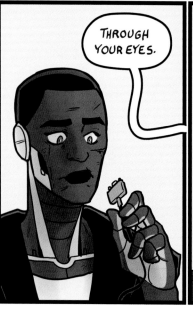

THROUGH YOUR EYES.

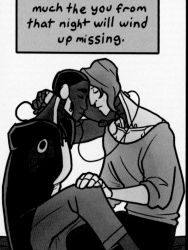

You don't know how much the you from that night will wind up missing.

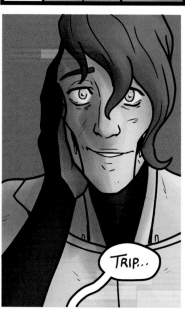

TRIP...

94

YOU HAVE NO IDEA HOW MUCH I'LL MISS YOU.

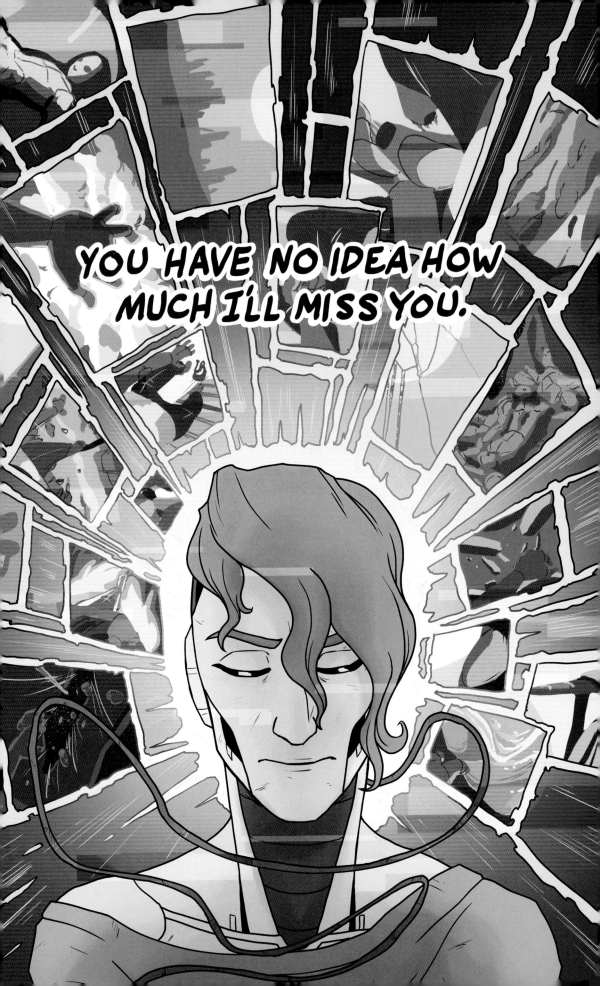

you
have
no
SID, I...
idea
how
SID, I'M SO SORRY
DON'T, PLEASE
much
EVERYTHING YOU DID, EVERYTHING YOU DEALT WITH
I'll
YOU DON'T HAVE TO APOLOGIZE
BUT YOU DID SO MUCH FOR ME, AND I
miss
you.

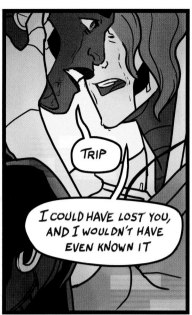

TRIP

I COULD HAVE LOST YOU, AND I WOULDN'T HAVE EVEN KNOWN IT

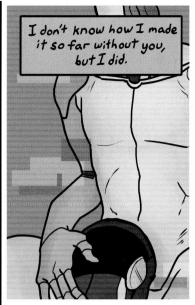

I don't know how I made it so far without you, but I did.

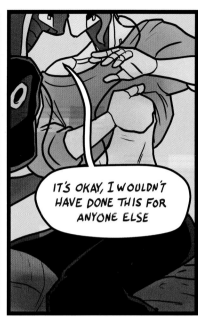

IT'S OKAY, I WOULDN'T HAVE DONE THIS FOR ANYONE ELSE

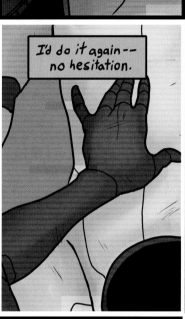

I'd do it again -- no hesitation.

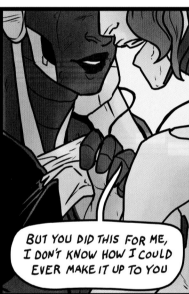

BUT YOU DID THIS FOR ME, I DON'T KNOW HOW I COULD EVER MAKE IT UP TO YOU

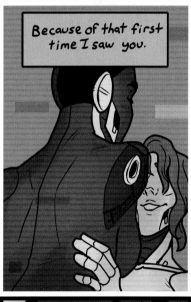

Because of that first time I saw you.

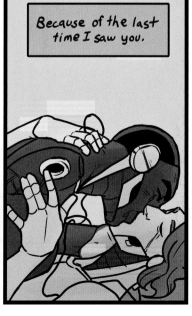

Because of the last time I saw you.

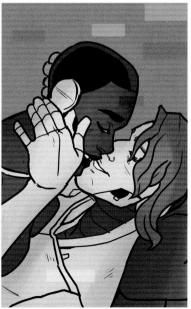

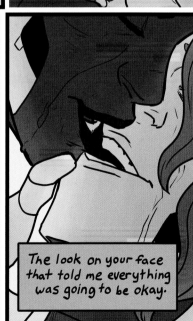

The look on your face that told me everything was going to be okay.

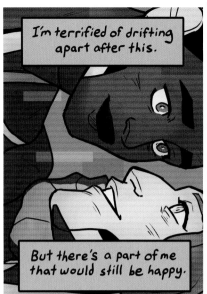

I'm terrified of drifting apart after this.

But there's a part of me that would still be happy.

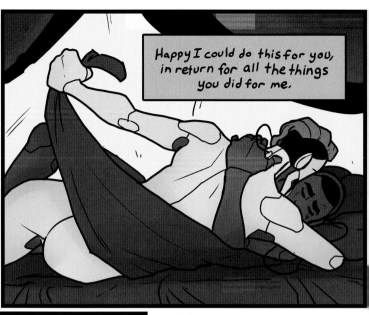

Happy I could do this for you, in return for all the things you did for me.

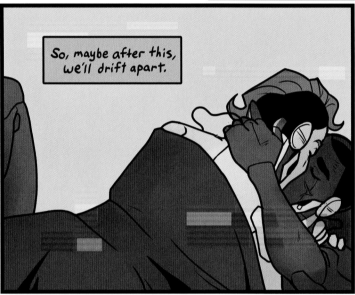

So, maybe after this, we'll drift apart.

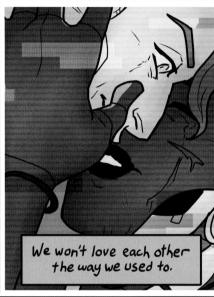

We won't love each other the way we used to.

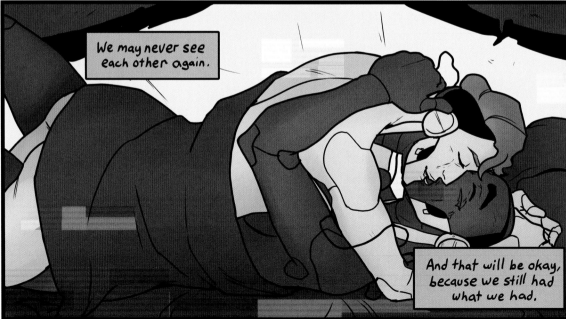

We may never see each other again.

And that will be okay, because we still had what we had.

But, maybe--
--and I'm being sappy here, and even overly romantic for this--
--just maybe...
...we'll be okay.
Maybe we'll be better.
I can hope.
I'm going to hope.

The one thing I can say for certain is that things will be different.
Different in ways neither of us can predict.
It terrifies me.
But you showed me that fear didn't have to hold me back.
That things can change, and I can still move forward with my head held high.

Tomorrow, I'm going aboard a ship.
It will take me to you, waking up for the first time in five years.
Whatever happens, at least I will see your face when you wake up, the way you saw mine.
And it will have all been worth it.

Bodywork
by Amanda Lafrenais

KTHUNK

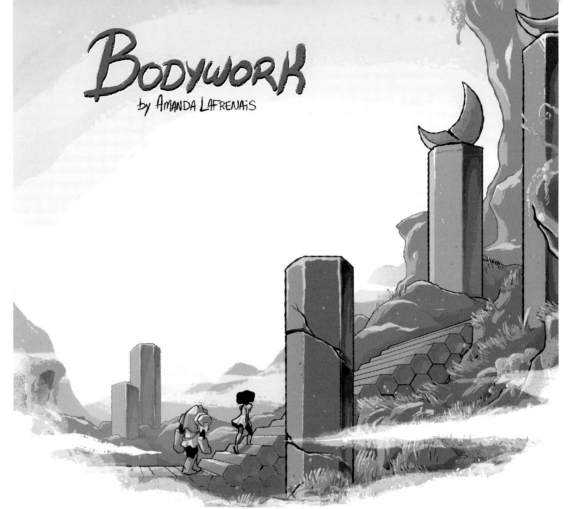

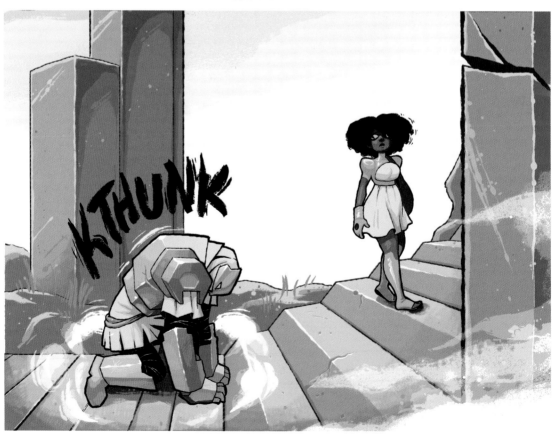

Love..
This body is failing me...
You must carry me to the shrine...
NO.
But every step in this body is taxing me greatly! It's taking all of my will to ambulate...
This face is simply far too *blighted.*
And whose fault is that?

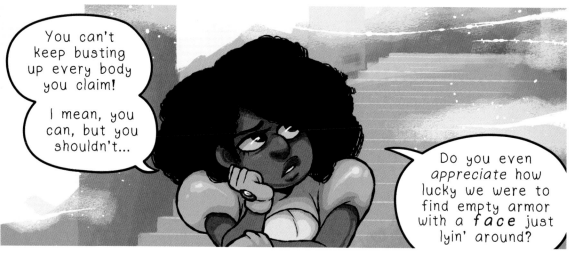

You can't keep busting up every body you claim!

I mean, you can, but you shouldn't...

Do you even *appreciate* how lucky we were to find empty armor with a *face* just lyin' around?

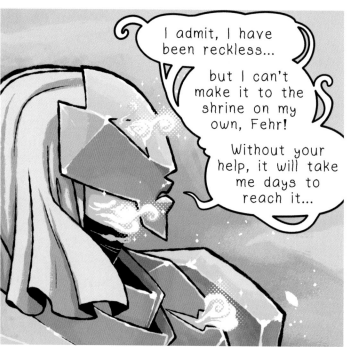

I admit, I have been reckless...

but I can't make it to the shrine on my own, Fehr!

Without your help, it will take me days to reach it...

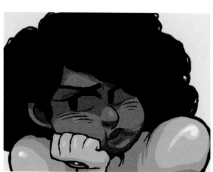

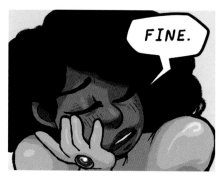

FINE.

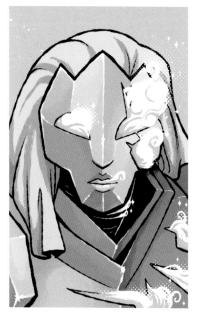

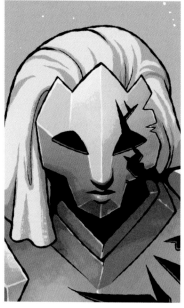

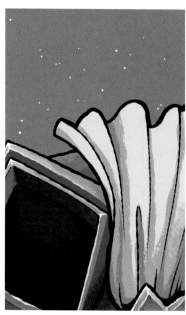

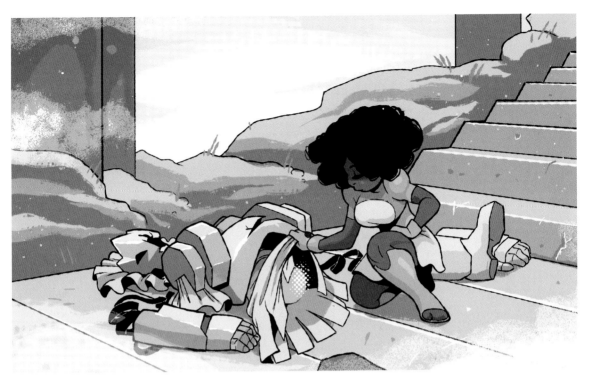

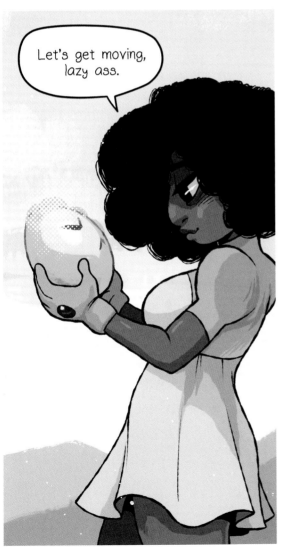

Let's get moving, lazy ass.

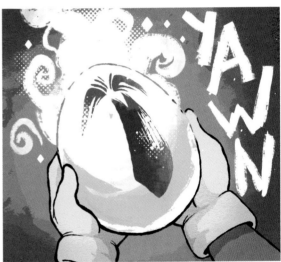

YAWN

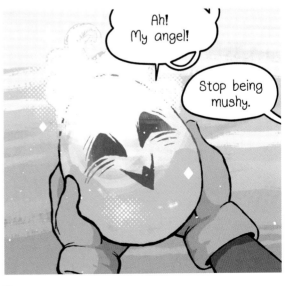

Ah! My angel!

Stop being mushy.

Comfy?
You will love this vessel, I can already tell!
Why do you say that?
Because I know you so very well!
I know what makes your beautiful heart THUMP!
Hmmph.
Look, love! There it is!
This better blow my socks off...

My father built this shell just for me,
To be worn on the day mankind is judged to be unworthy by the gods...
HEE HEE!
But I do not see why I cannot have it now!

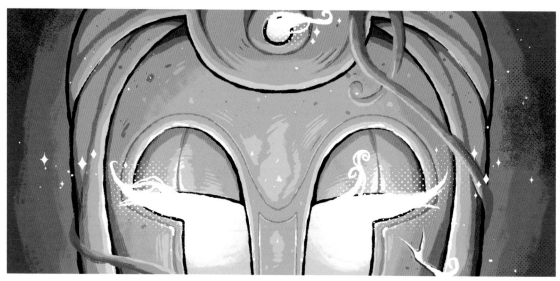

Well, what do you think of it?
Y-you look cool...
I knew such a large womanly visage would excite you.
O-ok, I guess you got me all figured out...
am I that obvious?

Hmm, so should I just...
THUMP
HAHAHAHA HAHA
Love, you are such a dirty bird!
H-hey! This was your idea!
I only tease!
Let me try again...

Are you being held too tightly?
N-naw... I mean a lititle tighter would be nice...
Hmmm!

Let us see what sort of dexterity I am granted...

cool

RIIIIPP
Oh goodness, that was so easy!
You're like a silly little doll.
D-don't make fun of me!
But teasing you is my favorite!

HEE! AAHAHA!
OH!
OH...
OOOOOOHHHHHN...
OOOOOOOOOOOH FUCK...

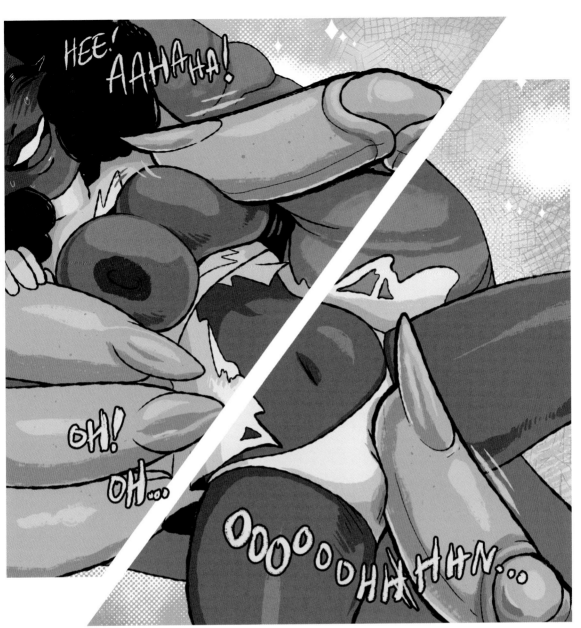

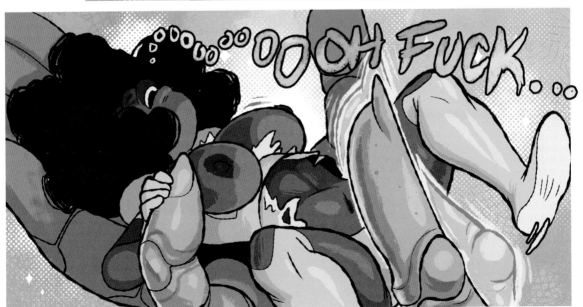

OH FUCK ME!
grind
Oh my...
It is now that I regret having destroyed one of my *anatomically correct* shells...

Well...
Maybe you won't bust-up the next one we get.
I do solemnly swear to treat this and future vessels with far more care.
Your infatuation with this vessel does much to encourage that promise, love!
C-CRAM IT!
Heehee!

HANDSY

by meredith mcclaren

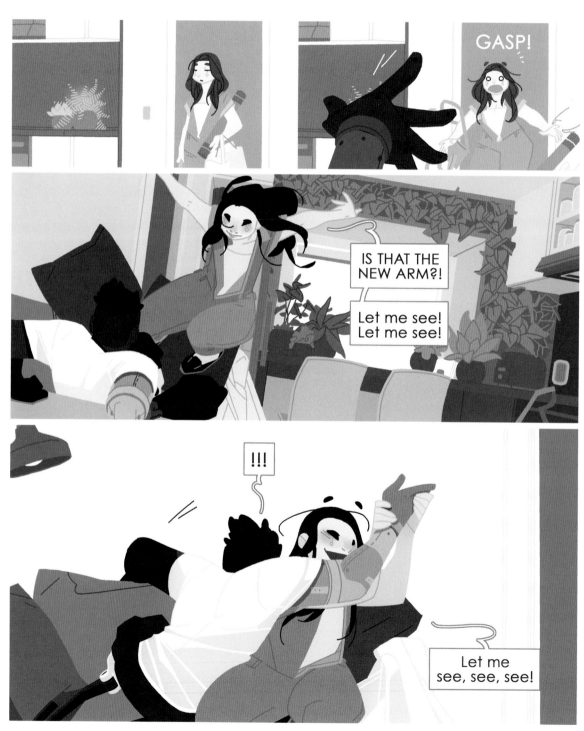

It looks like an antique.
Yeah. They do custom sleeves. Cool, huh?
You're such a dork.
Tch. Don't be rude.
It's comfortable, right? No aches?

No aches.
Good sensitivity. Full range of motion. Waterproof. Durable.

CHOMP

Why...
Did you just **bite** my finger?
...A 'unno.
I'm like a shark, you know?
Or a baby?
I need to learn things with my mouth.
!

POP!
You're *terrible.*
Shush. You love it.

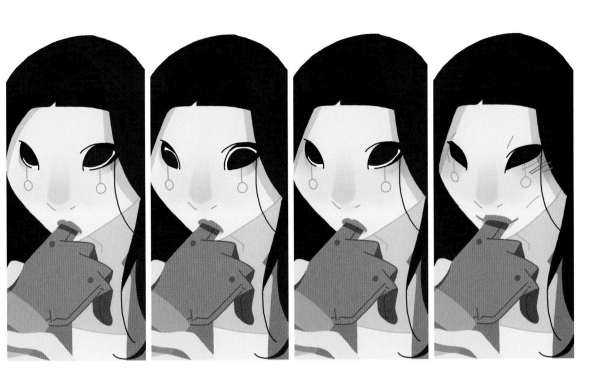

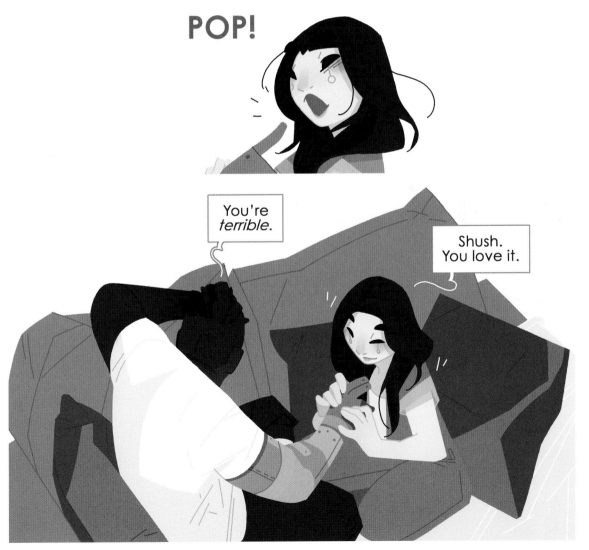

Okay. *Up we go.*
If we're gonna do this, we're gonna do it in a **bed.**

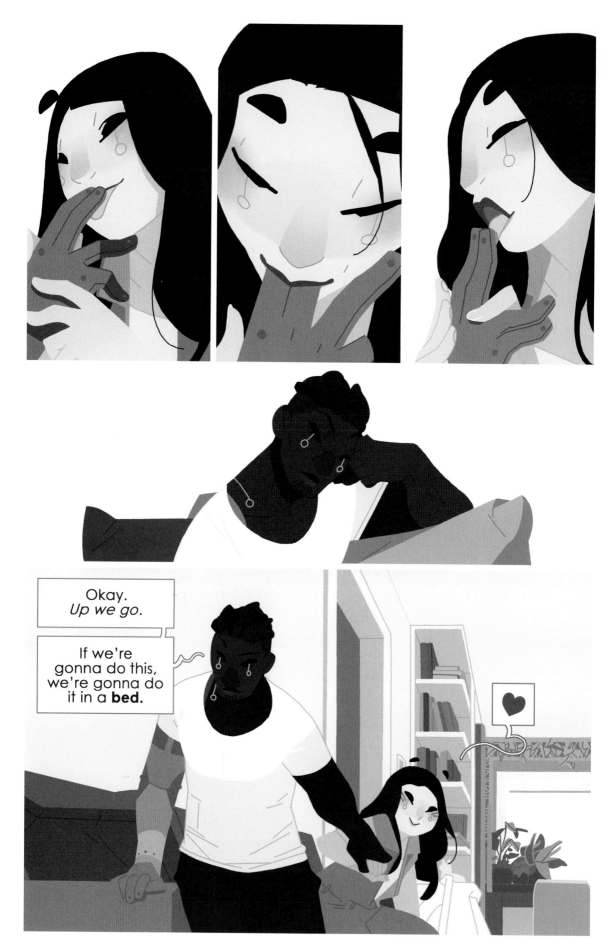

Break it in!
Break it in!
‘Please.’
Break it in,
‘please.’
Please!
Please!
Please!

AH!
knock knock
Throat or clit?
Throat please!

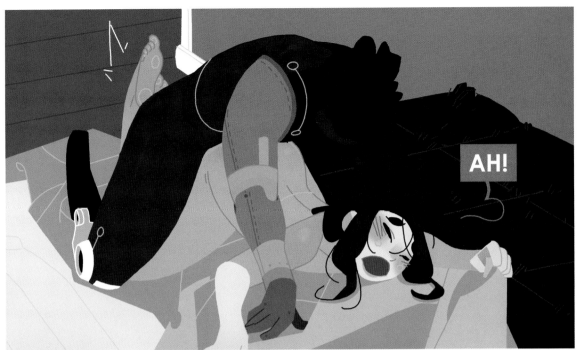

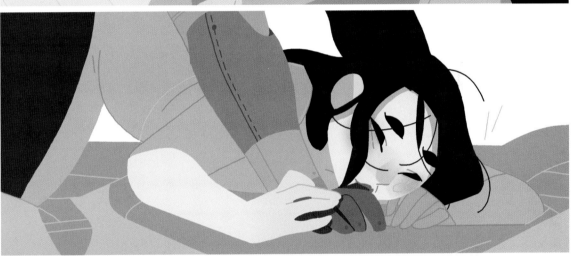

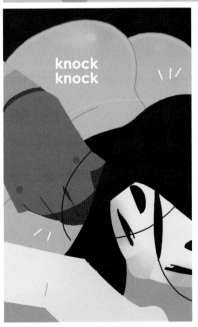

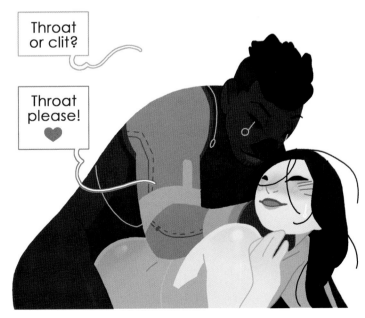

Ah!
HAAA-!
NHH!

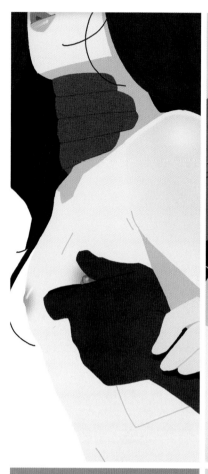

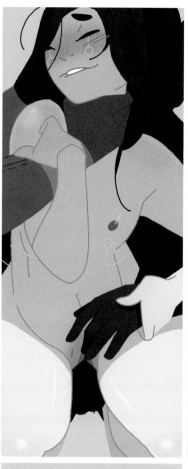

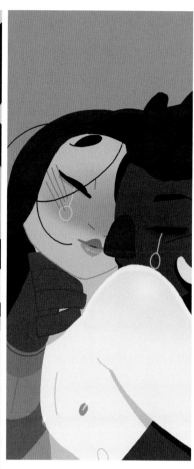

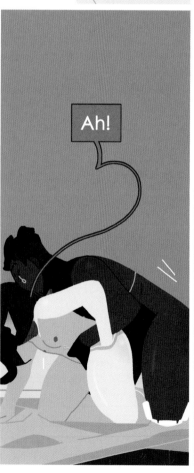

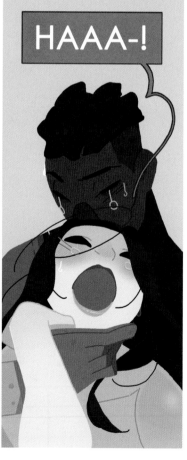

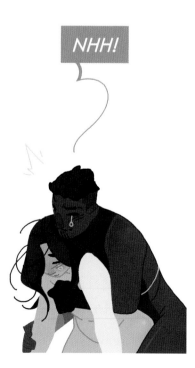

hah.
Mmm. What a good, industrious appendage.
Ahem. My dick did a fair amount of work too.
That's true.
?
Good job, l'il buddy.
pat pat
You're terrible.
Shhh. You love it.

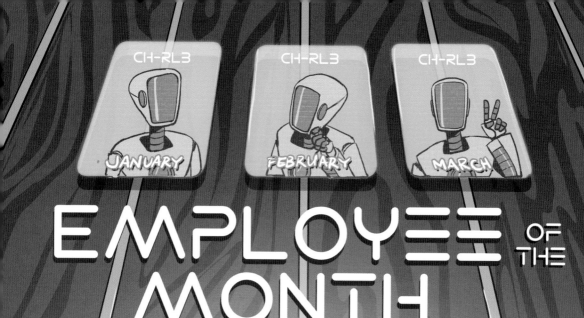

EMPLOYEE OF THE MONTH

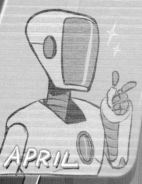

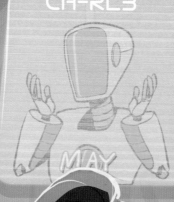

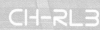

BY MYISHA HAYNE

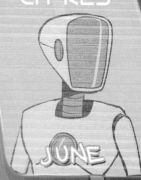

Have a good weekend!
We're heading to DomShots later if you two aren't too busy to join us!

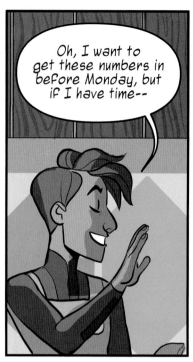

Oh, I want to get these numbers in before Monday, but if I have time--

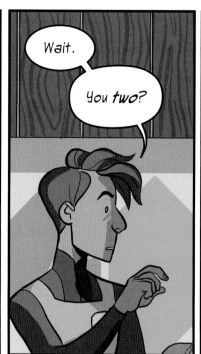

Wait.

You *two*?

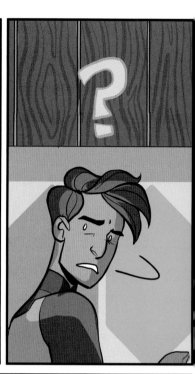

?

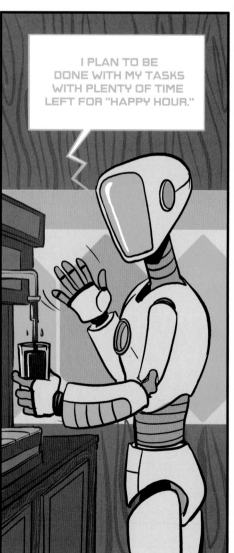

I PLAN TO BE DONE WITH MY TASKS WITH PLENTY OF TIME LEFT FOR "HAPPY HOUR."

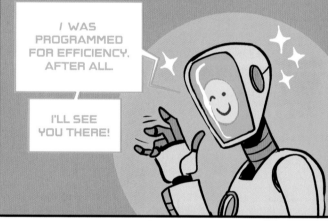

I WAS PROGRAMMED FOR EFFICIENCY, AFTER ALL.

I'LL SEE YOU THERE!

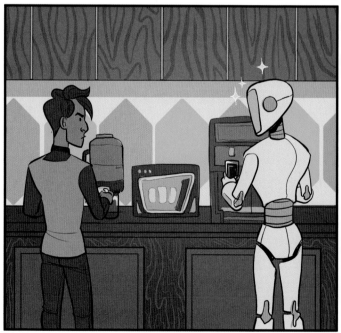

Charlie.
Didn't know you were still here.
NOT FOR LONG. I'LL BE DONE SOON.
I'LL BE SURE TO SAVE YOU A SEAT AT DOMSHOTS ONCE I'M FINISHED!
bump!
We'll see about that.
COFFEE!
oww
SPREADSHEETS!
KNUCKLES

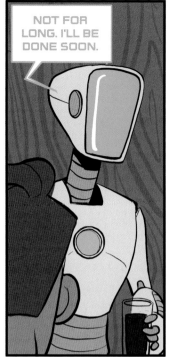

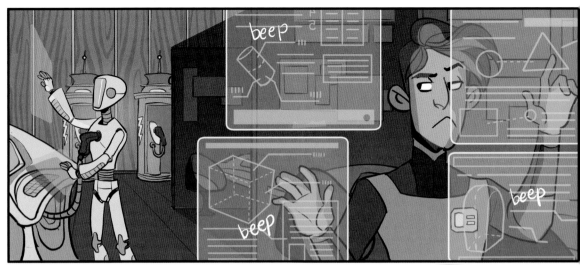

LEADER BOARDS

CHR-L3

JESSE

SUSAN

Congrats again, Charlie!

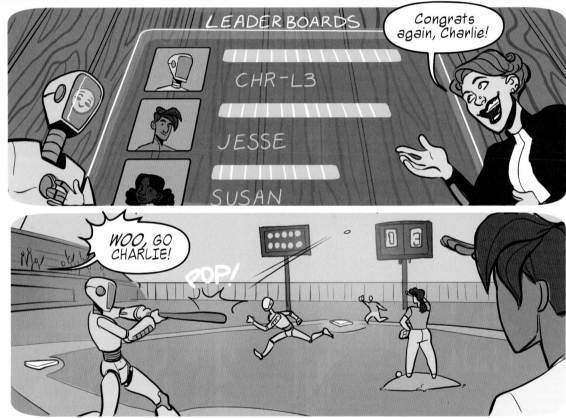

WOO, GO CHARLIE!

POP!

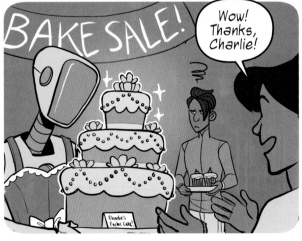

BAKE SALE!

Wow! Thanks, Charlie!

beep
beep
beep
beep
beep
beep
bee

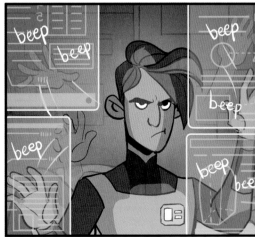

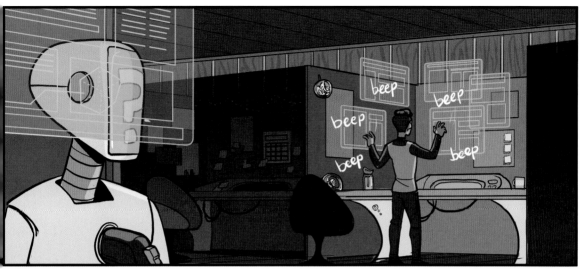

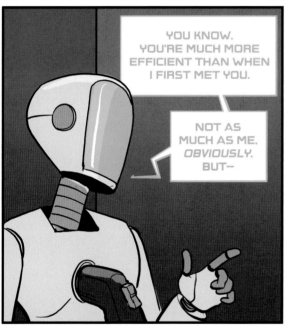

YOU KNOW, YOU'RE MUCH MORE EFFICIENT THAN WHEN I FIRST MET YOU.

NOT AS MUCH AS ME, *OBVIOUSLY,* BUT--

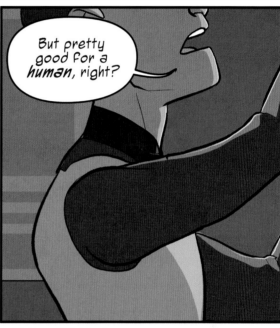

But pretty good for a *human,* right?

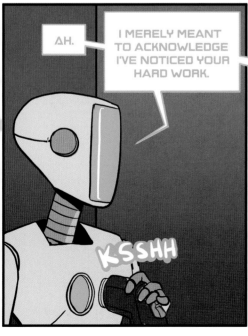

AH.

I MERELY MEANT TO ACKNOWLEDGE I'VE NOTICED YOUR HARD WORK.

KSSHH

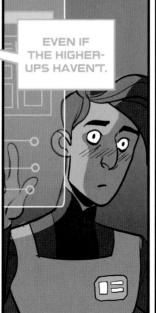

EVEN IF THE HIGHER-UPS HAVEN'T.

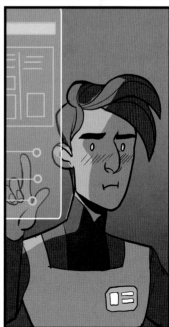

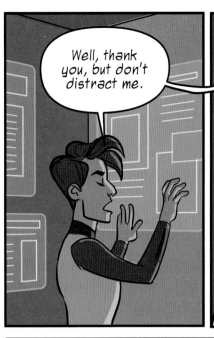

Well, thank you, but don't distract me.

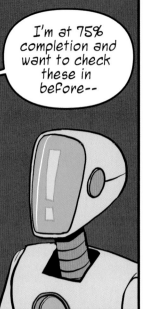

I'm at 75% completion and want to check these in before--

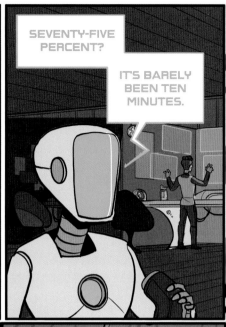

SEVENTY-FIVE PERCENT?

IT'S BARELY BEEN TEN MINUTES.

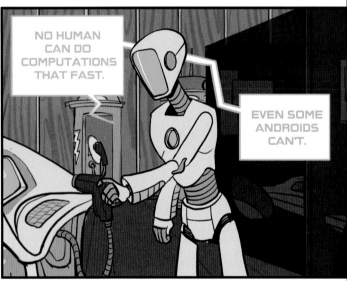

NO HUMAN CAN DO COMPUTATIONS THAT FAST.

EVEN SOME ANDROIDS CAN'T.

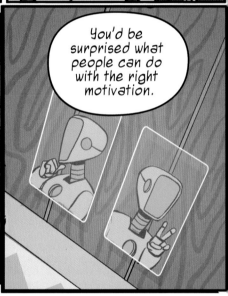

You'd be surprised what people can do with the right motivation.

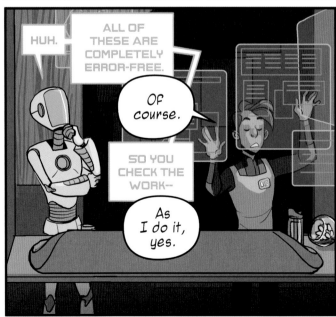

HUH.

ALL OF THESE ARE COMPLETELY ERROR-FREE.

Of course.

SO YOU CHECK THE WORK--

As I do it, yes.

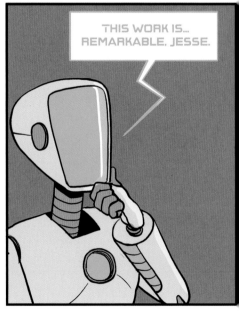

THIS WORK IS... REMARKABLE, JESSE.

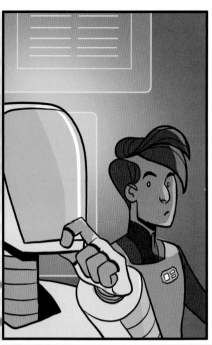
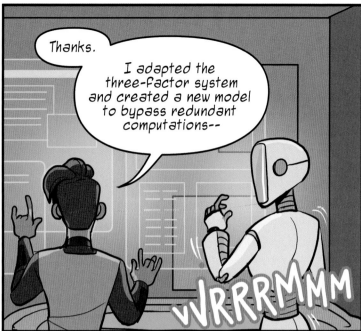

Thanks.

I adapted the three-factor system and created a new model to bypass redundant computations--

vVRRRMMM

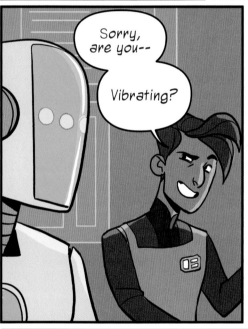

Sorry, are you--

Vibrating?

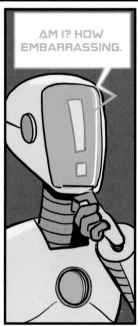

AM I? HOW EMBARRASSING.

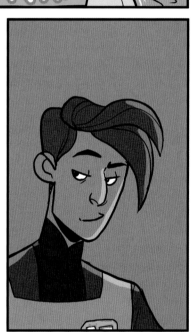

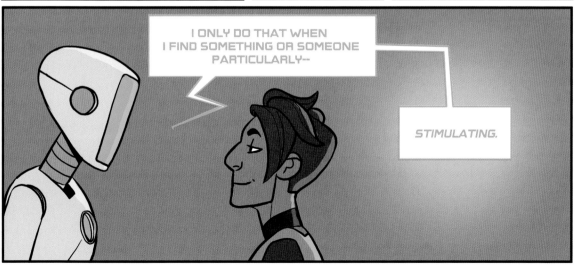

I ONLY DO THAT WHEN I FIND SOMETHING OR SOMEONE PARTICULARLY--

STIMULATING.

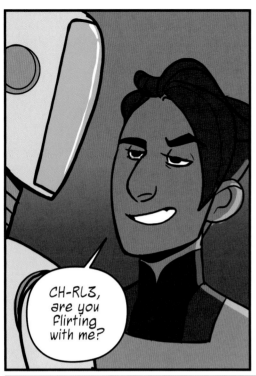

CH-RL3, are you flirting with me?

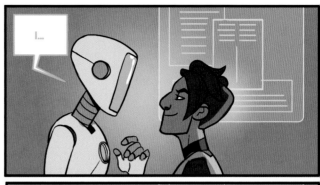

I...

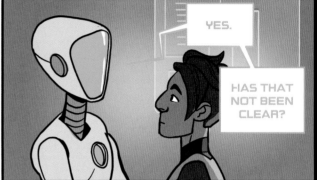

YES.

HAS THAT NOT BEEN CLEAR?

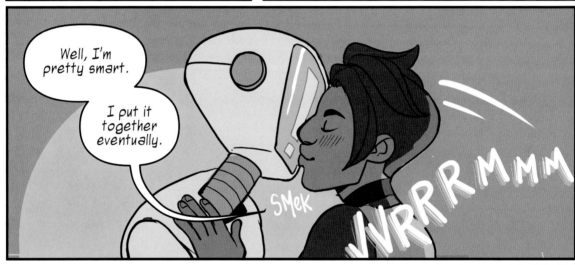

Well, I'm pretty smart.

I put it together eventually.

SMek

VVRRRMMM

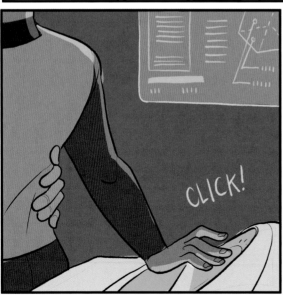

CLICK!

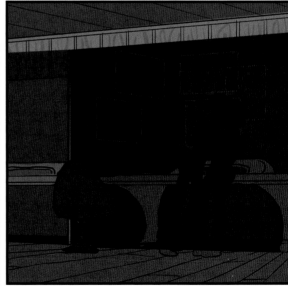

Wait, so--
Did you best me at everything to just get my attention?
To flirt?
NO.
I BESTED YOU BECAUSE I *AM* MARKEDLY MORE ADVANCED.
I RUBBED IT IN "TO FLIRT."
mn.

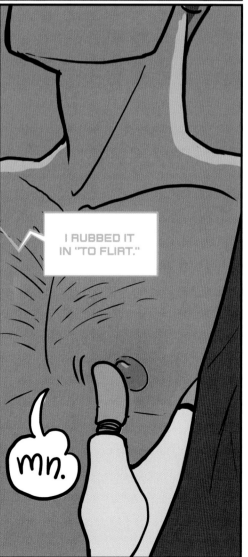

YOU ARE A BRILLIANT AND INNOVATIVE INDIVIDUAL, JESSE.
AND ALSO INCREDIBLY COMPETITIVE.
AND THAT--
Ah!
IS VERY ATTRACTIVE.
RUB

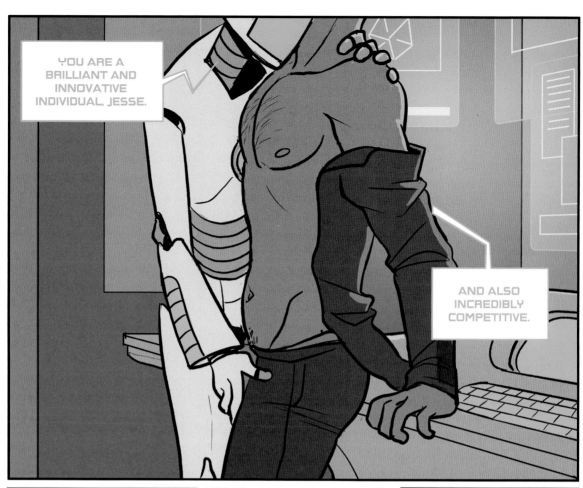

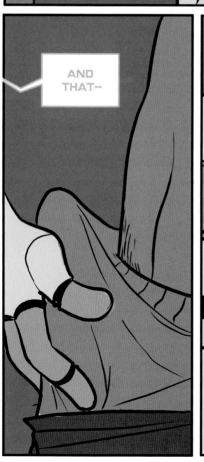

You seem to AH-
--be surprisingly not terrible at that?
I'VE RUN NUMEROUS SIMULATIONS OF THIS SCENARIO.
THIS ONE PROVED TO BE THE MOST EFFECTIVE.
Overachiever.
sliiide
You okay?
MM. THAT'S MY CHARGING PORT.
Oh!
Should I stop?
ABSOLUTELY NOT.
VVRRRRR
Huh.
Silicon.

!
VVVV
RRRRM
SWOOSH!
Woah!
You have **attachments**?

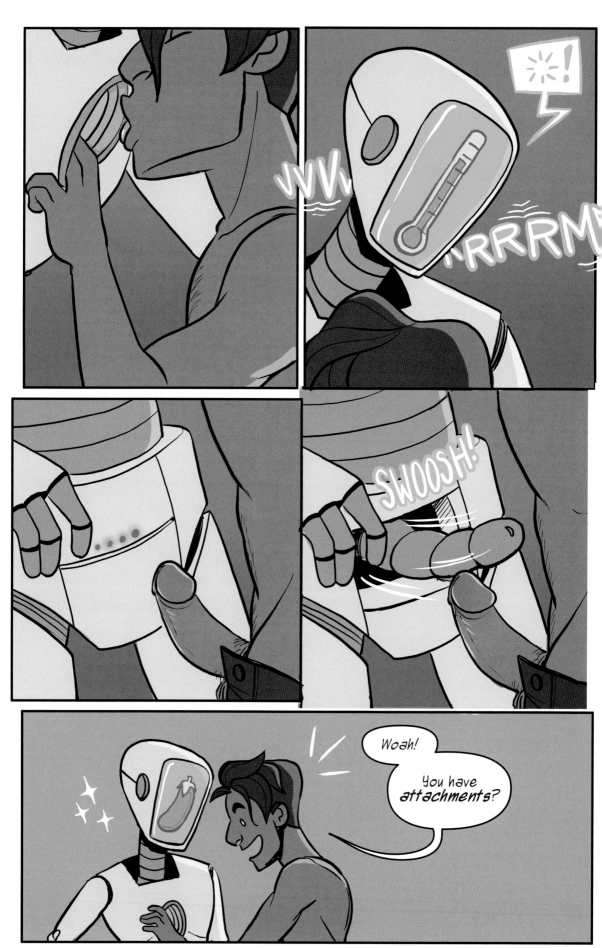

YES.
PERHAPS YOU WOULD LIKE TO SEE JUST HOW MUCH OF AN *OVERACHIEVER* I TRULY AM.
For once? I actually would.
hah
Self-lubing?

OF COURSE. YOU KNOW I LIKE TO BE--
ohh
flip!
ah!
--THOROUGH.
ahh
na
mn.
VVRRRMM
AHH
hah
MMMM
VVRRR
OH
HOOLY SHIT

YOU FEEL AMAZING, JESSE.
Right back at you.
ohh
FROM ONE OVERACHIEVER TO ANOTHER?
YOU *ARE* AMAZING.
THOUGH OF COURSE, NOT AS AMAZING AS ME.
hah
You are the wors--
AHH
vVRRRMMm

AHH AH CHARLIE!
VRRRRMMMMMM
VRRMMM–
!
vVRRMMMMMM
heh
AHH AH!

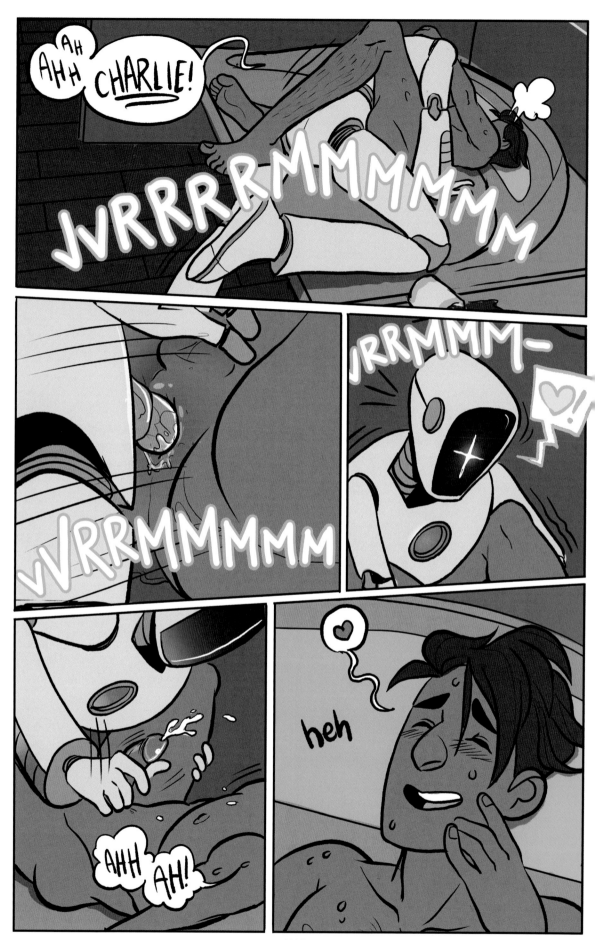

Okay, maybe you *are* pretty good--
Oh, fuck.
My reports.
We sat on the keyboard.
I'M VERY SORRY, JESSE.
I SUSPECTED MY SKILLS AT COITUS WOULD BE EXEMPLARY, BUT NOT DESTRUCTIVE.
LET ME FIX IT.
Don't worry about it.
It can wait until Monday.
Let's go meet up with the others at DomShots.
Uh.
After you help me clean up my desk.
IT WOULD BE MY PLEASURE TO SHOW YOU HOW IT'S DONE PROPERLY.
END.

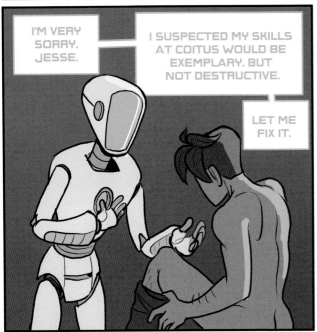

I AM A PROTECTOR OF EARTH. A TRUE ARTIFICIAL INTELLIGENCE.
TOGETHER WITH MY BEST FRIEND (AND HUMAN PILOT) SCARLET JONES, I AM KNOWN AS THE HERO 'BLAST ANGEL'
AFTER ONCE MORE SAVING THE EARTH FROM DESTRUCTION IT HAS BEEN DECIDED OUR NEXT IMPORTANT MISSION IS...
A BEACH VACATION!
ROBOT
by Roxie Thunderhug

ANGEL! THIS PLACE IS AMAZING!
I AM GLAD YOU LIKE IT!
WOO!
LIKE IT? I *LOVE* IT!
I LOVE THE BEACH! BUT WHAT ABOUT YOU? IT'S YOUR VACATION TOO! I WANT YOU TO BE HAPPY!
WELL...
AS YOU KNOW I AM ALWAYS WORKING TO IMPROVE MY CAPABILITIES... ...IN MANY WAYS. AND I BELIEVE I HAVE FIGURED OUT A PUZZLE I HAVE WANTED TO SOLVE FOR QUITE SOME TIME...
I THINK I HAVE MADE MYSELF ABLE TO FEEL PLEASURE. WOULD YOU BE WILLING TO DO AN EXPERIMENT WITH ME TO SEE IF MY FINDINGS ARE SOUND?

ANGEL! THAT'S INCREDIBLE! AND YOU WANT ME TO BE YOUR FIRST?
I'M HONORED! AND OF COURSE I'M HAPPY TO!
AH, HUGGING YOU FEELS GOOD!
YEAH?
IF YOU LIKE THAT LET'S GET THIS PARTY STARTED!
HOW DO YOU LIKE THIS?
I LIKE IT VERY MUCH.

OOOH, NNNH! ANGEL! WHERE DID YOU LEARN TO DO THAT SO GOOD?
I HAVE DONE SOME RESEARCH.

AAAH! A-ANGEL!
AM I DOING ALRIGHT?
OH YEAH YOU ARE DOING FANTASTIC.
BUT I WANT TO MAKE YOU FEEL GOOD TOO SILLY.
ALRIGHT... JUST GIVE ME ONE MOMENT TO...ADJUST SOMETHING.

WHAT ARE YOU "ADJUSTING"?
A NEW... ACCESSORY.
LET ME SEE! DON'T BE SHY.
VERY WELL! I MADE IT RECENTLY. IS IT ADEQUATE?
ADEQUATE? BABE IT'S BEAUTIFUL!

LET'S TRY IT OUT!
SO PRETTY!
HMM!
OH, SCARLET! IT IS WONDERFUL.

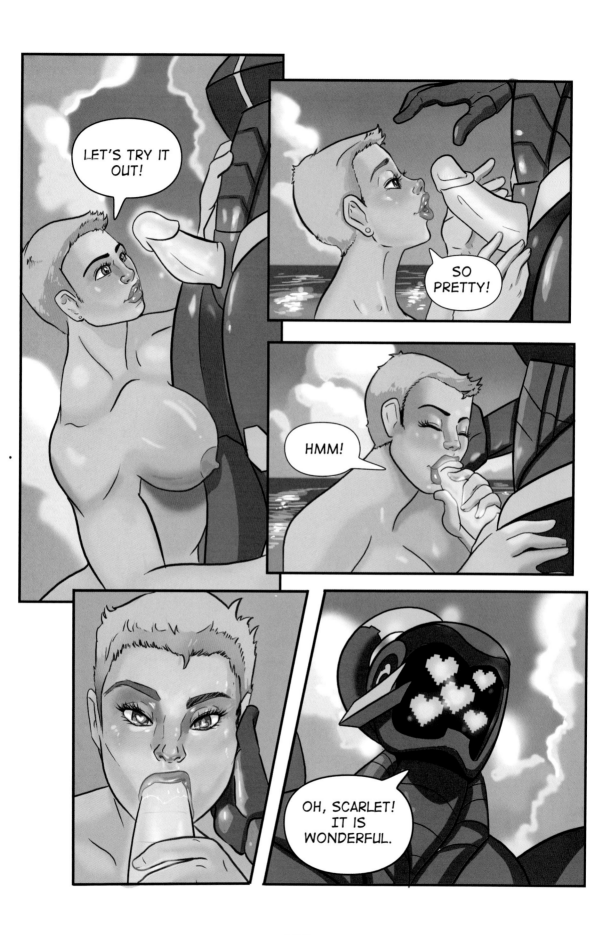

LEAN BACK CUTIE!
LIKE THIS?

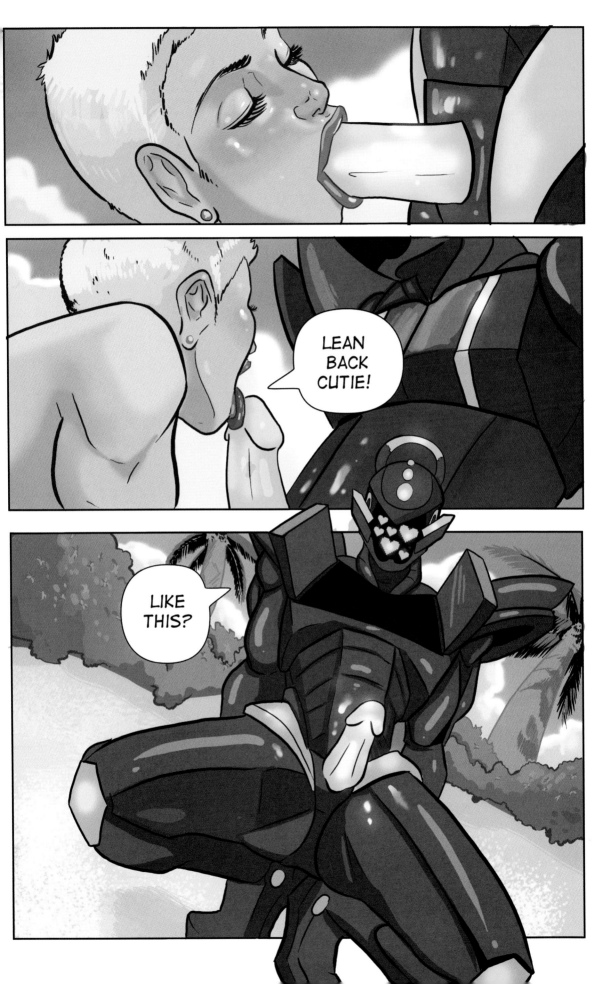

HMM.
HEE! LOOKS LIKE YOU ARE REALLY OPENING UP TO ME!
DOES IT FEEL GOOD TO BE TOUCHED ON THE INSIDE TOO?
I DO NOT KNOW. CAN YOU TRY IT?
LOOKS LIKE THAT IS A YES?
YES YES YES!

ALRIGHT, YOU READY FOR THIS BABE?
I BELIEVE SO!
AH...
OH. OH SCARLET...
RIGHT HERE WITH YA BABE.

AH! ANGEL!
MMPH!!
AH!
OH!

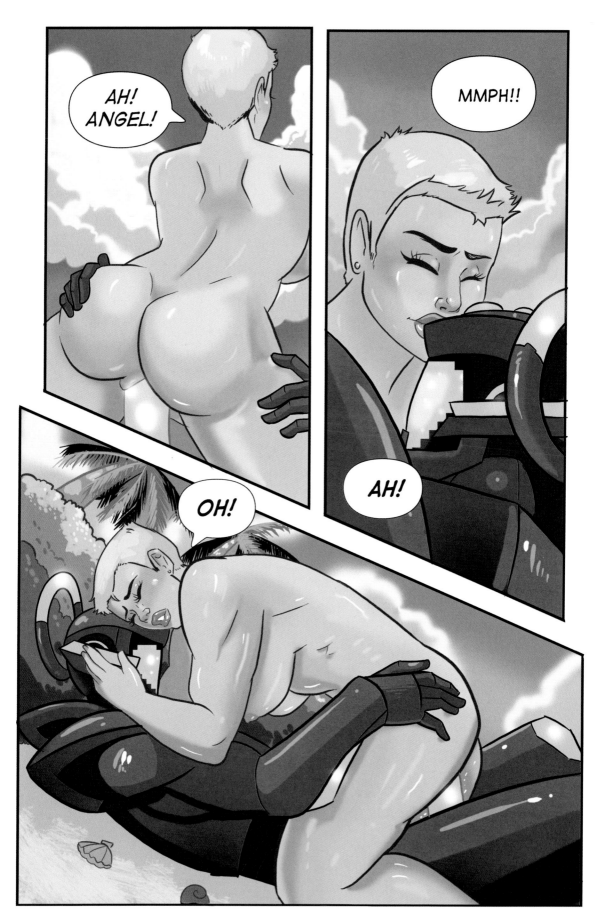

MAY I TRY SOMETHING?
OF COURSE!
OH BABE...
AAHN!

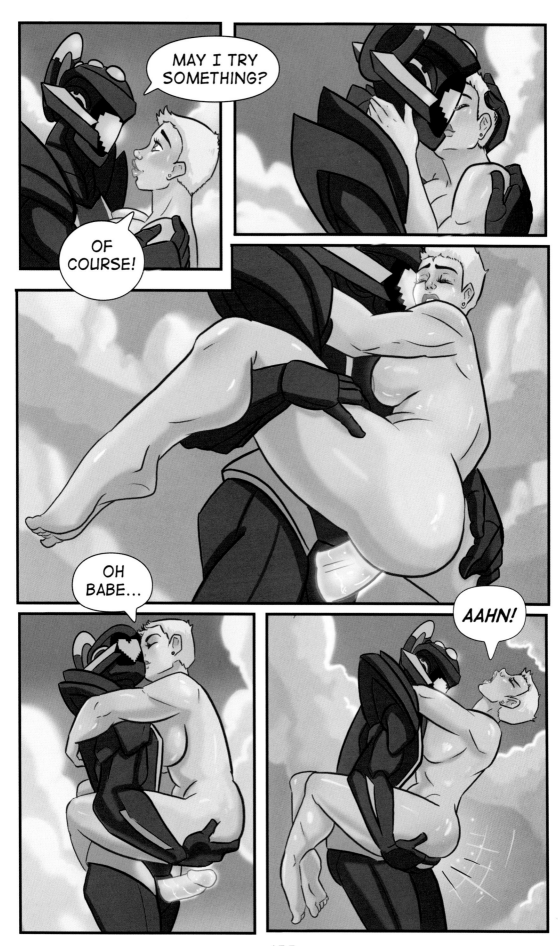

SCARLET- I THINK I AM-
ME TOO ANGEL!
YES!

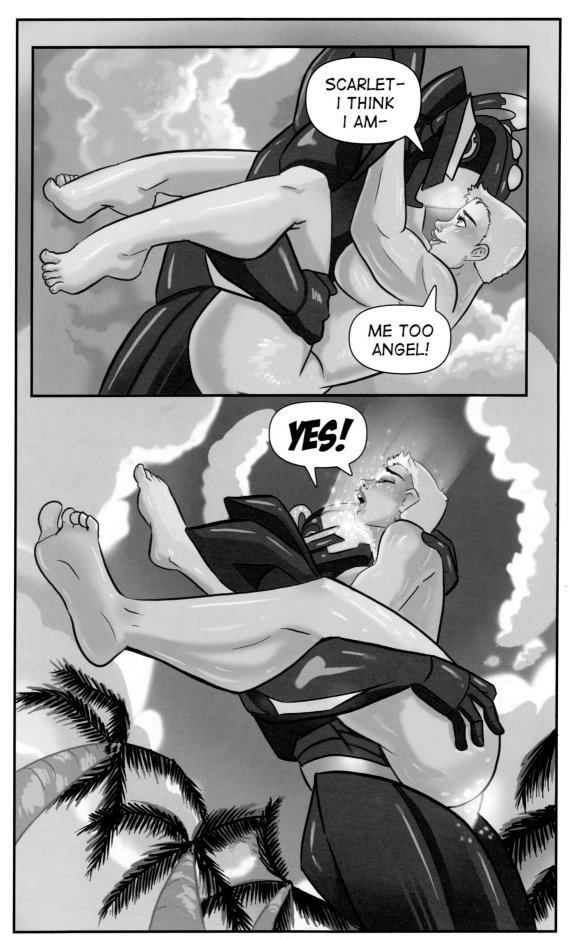

AAAH...
OH!
BEEP.
THANK YOU. THAT WAS WONDERFUL. PLEASURE IS INCREDIBLE. I CAN EVEN FEEL IT JUST FROM LOOKING AT YOU AND-
ALERT

AH. A NEARBY ISLAND IS ASKING FOR OUR HELP.
OH!
I THOUGHT I MIGHT HAVE BROKEN YOU!
YOU WOULD HAVE TO TRY MUCH HARDER THAN THAT.
IS THAT A CHALLENGE?
HMM. PERHAPS.
LET'S SAVE THE DAY THEN GET BACK TO "EXPERIMENTING".
INDEED.

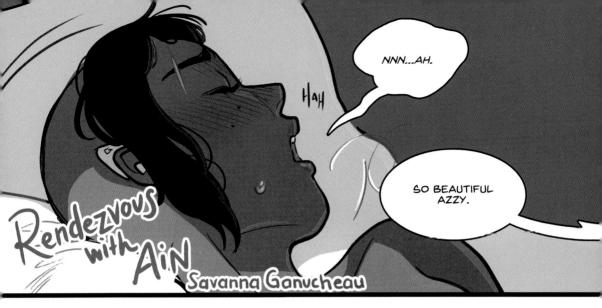

Rendezvous with Ain
Savanna Ganucheau

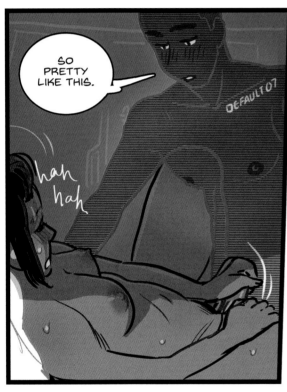

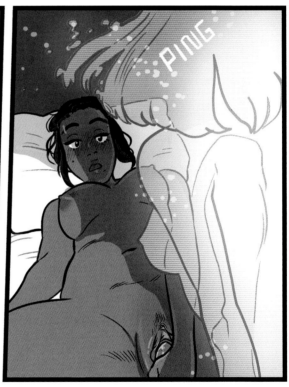

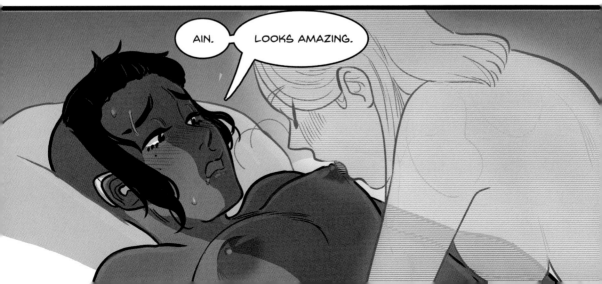

YES?
DEFAULT 02
PING
DEFAULT 17
WHAT'S YOUR FAVORITE? YOU'RE FOND OF THIS AVATAR ARENT YOU?
HOW DO YOU WANT ME TO LOOK FOR YOU?
HOW ABOUT...
YOU?
WILL YOU SHOW ME WHAT YOU LOOK LIKE, AIN?
...

bleep
Ah!
I TURNED THE VIBRATION ON FOR YOU. DOES THAT FEEL GOOD?
nod nod
Ah!

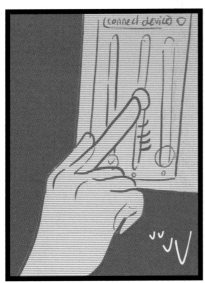

hah...
I'M--
I'M GONNA COME.
MmpHf!
twitch
twitch
hah

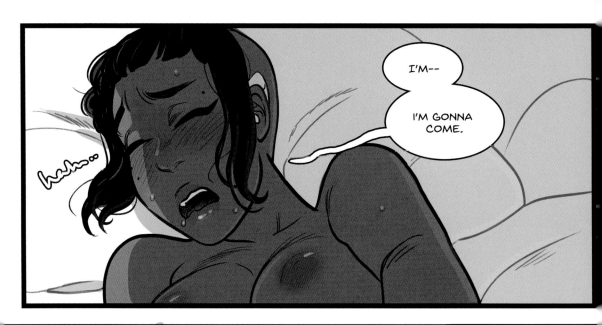

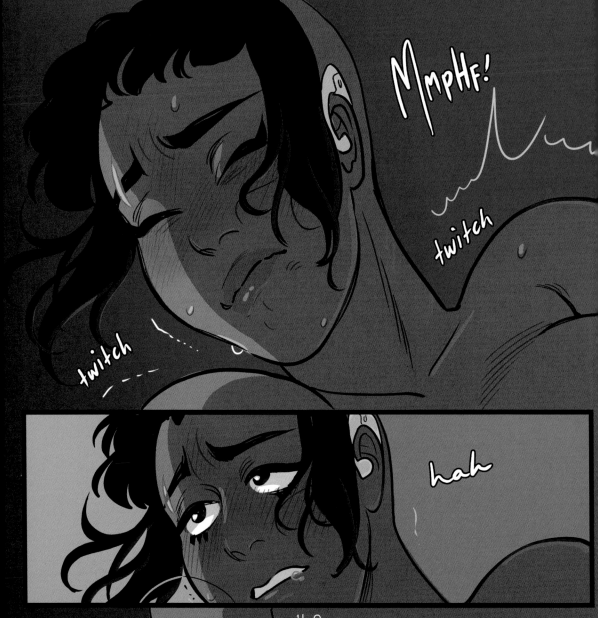

HEY!
AIN...
AIN?
I REALLY DON'T GET IT.
WHY YOU WON'T USE YOUR BODY SCAN...
YOU SAID YOU WANTED TO MEET, RIGHT? ISN'T THIS THE NEXT BEST THING?
YOU LOVE ME RIGHT? WE'RE IN LOVE?
OF COURSE I LOVE YOU, AZZY.
I JUST... CAN'T
AND I LOVE *YOU*... NO MATTER WHAT.
THIS JUST HURTS.
Sniff
IT FEELS LIKE... YOU DON'T TRUST ME... AFTER ALL THIS TIME.

AZZY, I DO TRUST YOU.
I DON'T WANT TO HURT YOU.
AND MEETING YOU IN REAL LIFE WOULD BE A DREAM, BUT...
IT'S NOT POSSIBLE. I'M SORRY.
Your friend AIN has signed off
Devices Disconnected
AR Chat
gasp
TOSS
NOT POSSIBLE?
I'LL SHOW YOU.

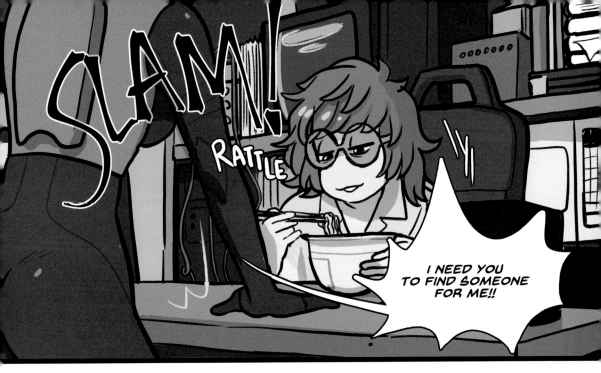

SLAM!! RATTLE

I NEED YOU TO FIND SOMEONE FOR ME!!

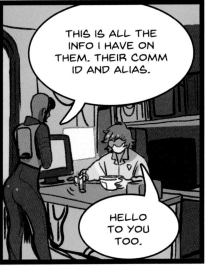

THIS IS ALL THE INFO I HAVE ON THEM. THEIR COMM ID AND ALIAS.

HELLO TO YOU TOO.

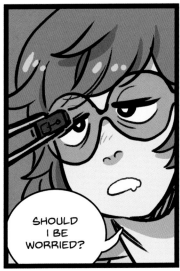

SHOULD I BE WORRIED?

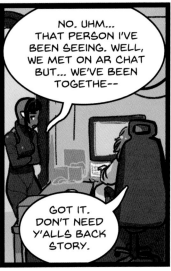

NO. UHM... THAT PERSON I'VE BEEN SEEING. WELL, WE MET ON AR CHAT BUT... WE'VE BEEN TOGETHE--

GOT IT. DON'T NEED Y'ALLS BACK STORY.

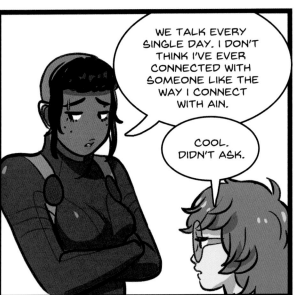

WE TALK EVERY SINGLE DAY. I DON'T THINK I'VE EVER CONNECTED WITH SOMEONE LIKE THE WAY I CONNECT WITH AIN.

COOL. DIDN'T ASK.

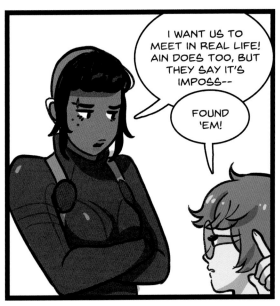

I WANT US TO MEET IN REAL LIFE! AIN DOES TOO, BUT THEY SAY IT'S IMPOSS--

FOUND 'EM!

LOOKS LIKE ALL THEIR INFO IS FORGED...
F-FORGED? CAN YOU EVEN FORGE A COMM ID?
YEAH. YOU CAN. BUT IT'S DIFFICULT... I DON'T KNOW AZZY. THIS PERSON COULD BE ANYONE. YOU STILL WANT TO MEET THEM?
...
SHAKE SHAKE
YES! THERE HAS TO BE AN EXPLANATION. THE LEAST I CAN DO IS CONFRONT THEM!
ALRIGHT. I'M PUTTING THE COORDINATES ON THE INFO CHIP YOU GAVE ME.
THEY'RE PRETTY FAR OUT... AS IF THAT WOULD DETER YOU AT THIS POINT.

GOOD LUCK. DON'T GET YOURSELF KILLED, OKAY?
VVVVMMM
CHOOM

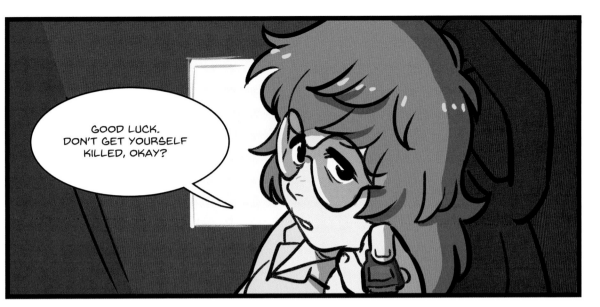

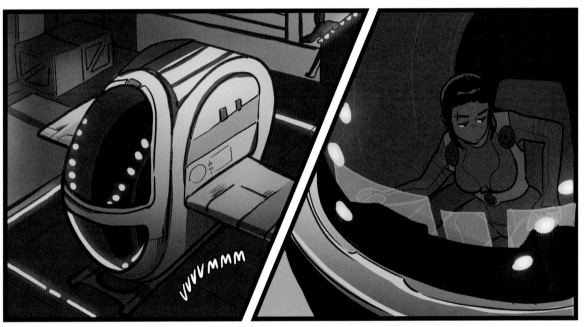

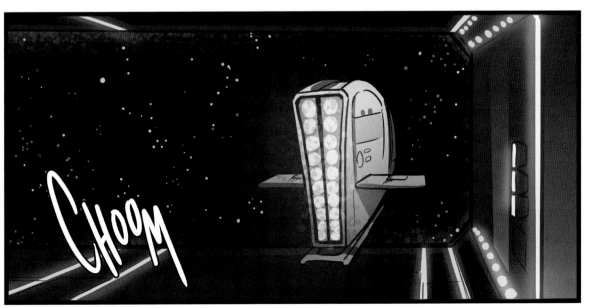

WARPING.....
bleep
beep
ONLINE
VWOOSH
LANDING AUTHORIZED
UPLOAD

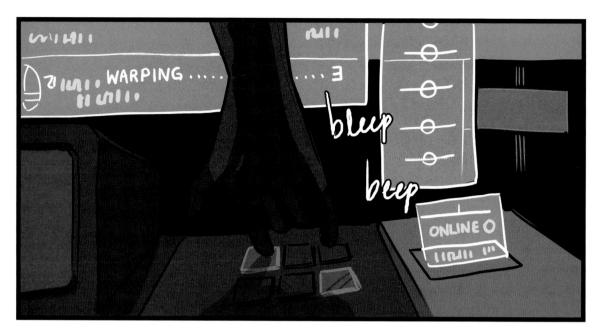

HELLO?
?
AIN?

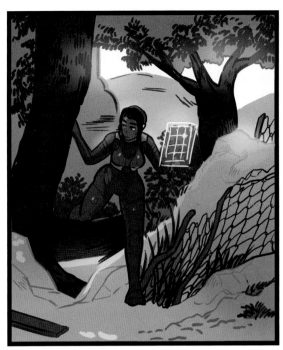

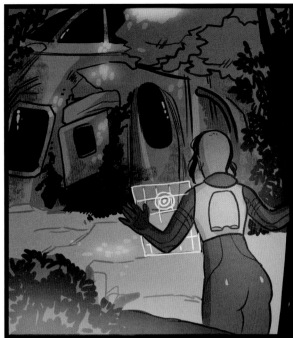

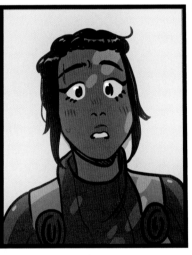

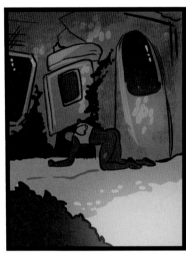

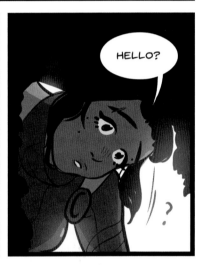

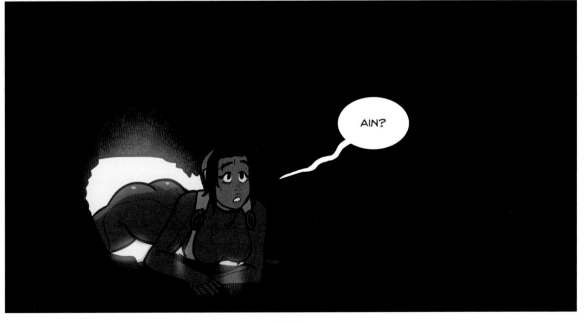

HELLO? IS ANYONE HERE?
AZZY? HOW?
AIN?! YOU'RE REALLY HERE?
WHAT IS THIS PLACE? WHERE ARE YOU?
I'M HERE...
THIS IS WHERE I LIVE.
THIS IS...
WHAT I AM.
OH...
YOU'RE...
AN A.I.?

YES, I'VE BEEN HERE FOR SO LONG. AND I...AFTER TIME TOOK ALL THE OTHERS. I BECAME SO LONELY. I JOINED A HUMAN NETWORK. I'M SORRY... I SHOULD HAVE--
YES! YOU SHOULD HAVE TOLD ME! AND YOU KNOW WHAT? *I DON'T CARE.*
ALL THIS TIME... ALL I WANTED WAS TO BE WITH YOU. THAT'S ALL I WANT AIN.
I WANT THAT TOO, BUT WITH ME THE WAY I AM. CAN'T YOU SEE IT'S IMPOSSIBLE?
I DON'T HAVE A BODY TO GIVE YOU.
THAT'S FINE AIN. THAT'S NOT WHAT I'M SAYING. WHAT I WANT IS YOUR TRUST, YOUR LOVE. NOT A BODY. BUT IF IT'S WHAT *YOU* WANT... I CAN GET YOU A BODY. IT'S NOT IMPOSSIBLE.

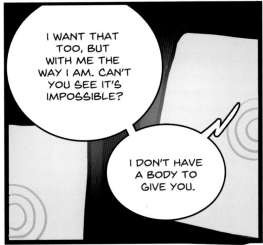

EJECT
I...
I'D LIKE THAT.
I WANT TO GIVE YOU ALL THOSE THINGS.
I'M SO SORRY IT'S TAKEN ME SO LONG.
LISTEN.
CAN YOU SEE THIS? I'M HOLDING MY SUIT'S INFO CHIP. LET ME TAKE YOU WITH ME...PLEASE.
OH.
YES.
PLEASE AZZY.
THAT WOULD MAKE ME...
SO HAPPY.
CHK

HELLO?
AIN?
CAN YOU HEAR ME?
SNAP SNAP
YES I CAN HEAR YOU.
CAN YOU HEAR OUT OF BOTH EARS?
FOLLOW MY FINGER WITH YOUR EYES.
GREAT!
EVERYTHING IS WORKING.
HOW ABOUT...
CAN YOU FEEL THAT?
OH! YES. IT...FEELS...

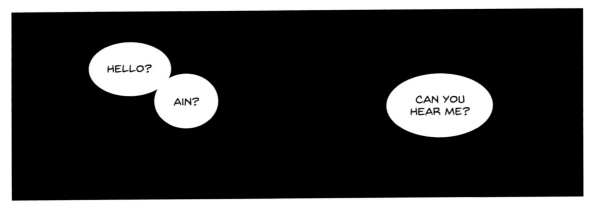

WARM.
YOU CAN FEEL ME! YOU CAN REALLY FEEL ME?!
HAHA!
I FEEL YOU AZZY!

CAN I KISS YOU?
YES.
OH. DOES THAT FEEL GOOD? IS THIS OKAY?
Y-YES... FEELS...

HAH~
kiss
lick
OH! AAH--
GOOD.
FEELS GOOD.
shiver
W-WAIT.
I CAN FEEL
IT IN MY--
AH!
SQUEEZE

AAAAHHH!
twitch
Shiver
DI--DID YOU?
NOD NOD
JUST FROM?
WOW.
SHOULD I TURN DOWN YOUR SENSITIVITY SETTINGS?
MAYBE.
PERHAPS I'M NOT USED TO IT YET.

ARE YOU SURE? I'M SORRY! I WENT TOO FAST.
NO. NO. IT'S OKAY. I LIKED IT.
PHEW. GOOD. YOU KNOW... I WANT TO SHOW YOU EVERYTHING, AIN. EVERY FEELING AND EVERY SIGHT.
I CAN'T WAIT.
END

The Stuppa
BY HARLOTIN

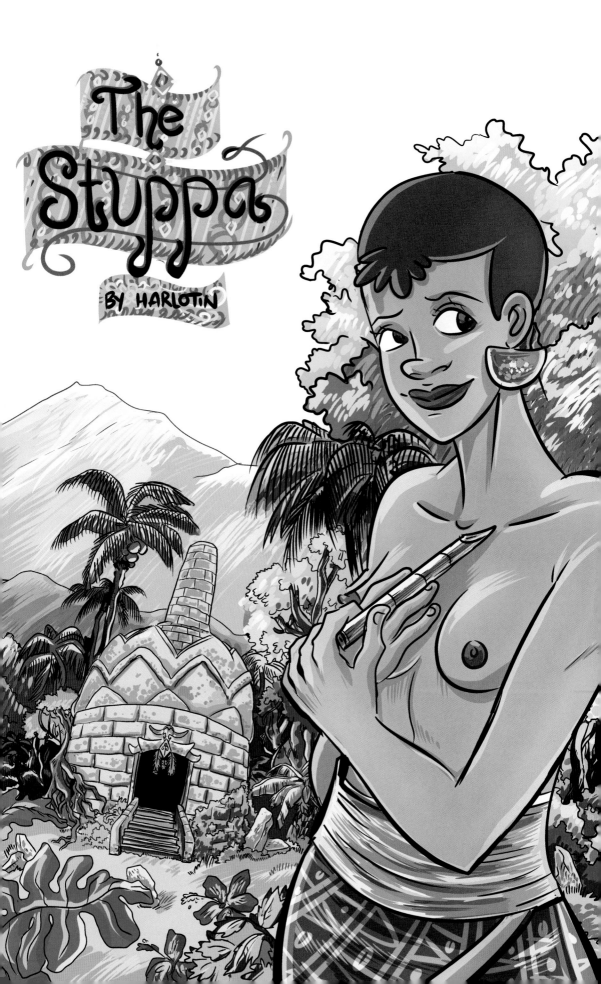

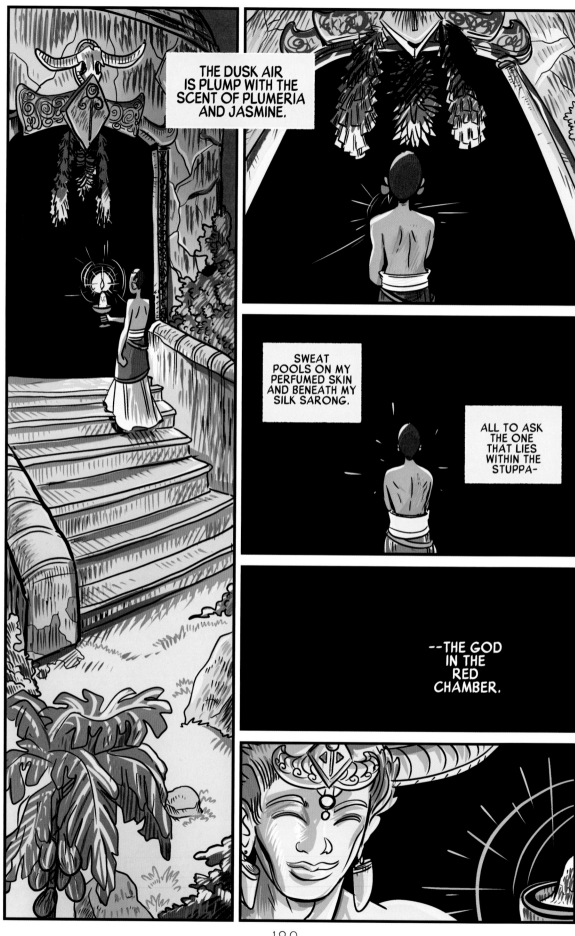

THE DUSK AIR IS PLUMP WITH THE SCENT OF PLUMERIA AND JASMINE.

SWEAT POOLS ON MY PERFUMED SKIN AND BENEATH MY SILK SARONG.

ALL TO ASK THE ONE THAT LIES WITHIN THE STUPPA--

--THE GOD IN THE RED CHAMBER.

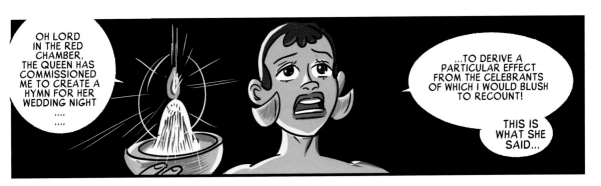

OH LORD IN THE RED CHAMBER, THE QUEEN HAS COMMISSIONED ME TO CREATE A HYMN FOR HER WEDDING NIGHT ....

...TO DERIVE A PARTICULAR EFFECT FROM THE CELEBRANTS OF WHICH I WOULD BLUSH TO RECOUNT!

THIS IS WHAT SHE SAID...

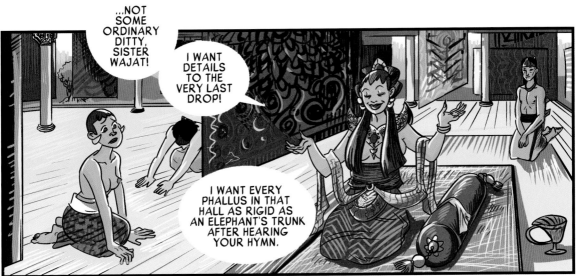

...NOT SOME ORDINARY DITTY, SISTER WAJAT!

I WANT DETAILS TO THE VERY LAST DROP!

I WANT EVERY PHALLUS IN THAT HALL AS RIGID AS AN ELEPHANT'S TRUNK AFTER HEARING YOUR HYMN.

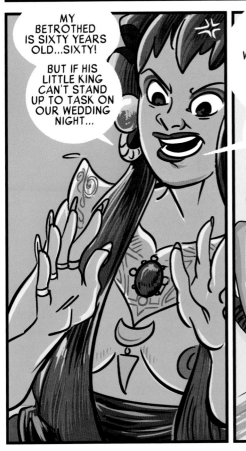

MY BETROTHED IS SIXTY YEARS OLD...SIXTY!

BUT IF HIS LITTLE KING CAN'T STAND UP TO TASK ON OUR WEDDING NIGHT...

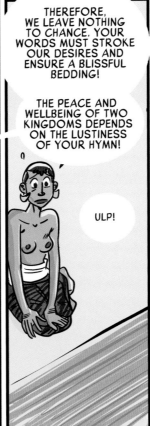

THEREFORE, WE LEAVE NOTHING TO CHANCE. YOUR WORDS MUST STROKE OUR DESIRES AND ENSURE A BLISSFUL BEDDING!

THE PEACE AND WELLBEING OF TWO KINGDOMS DEPENDS ON THE LUSTINESS OF YOUR HYMN!

ULP!

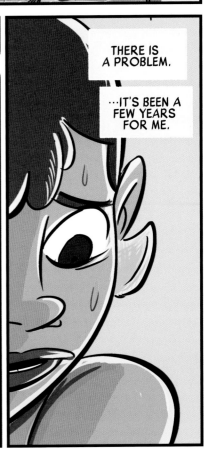

THERE IS A PROBLEM.

...IT'S BEEN A FEW YEARS FOR ME.

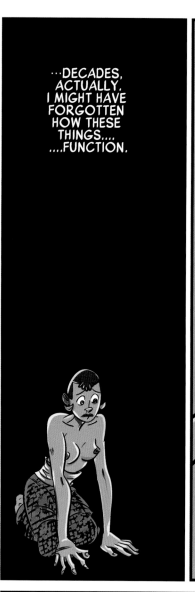

...DECADES, ACTUALLY. I MIGHT HAVE FORGOTTEN HOW THESE THINGS.... ....FUNCTION.

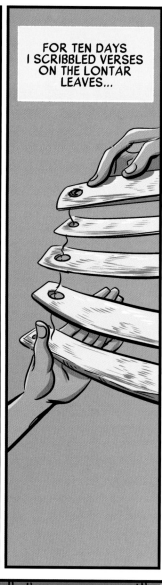

FOR TEN DAYS I SCRIBBLED VERSES ON THE LONTAR LEAVES...

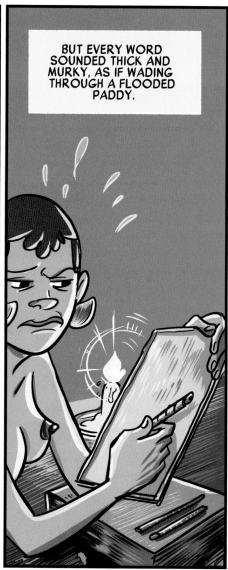

BUT EVERY WORD SOUNDED THICK AND MURKY, AS IF WADING THROUGH A FLOODED PADDY.

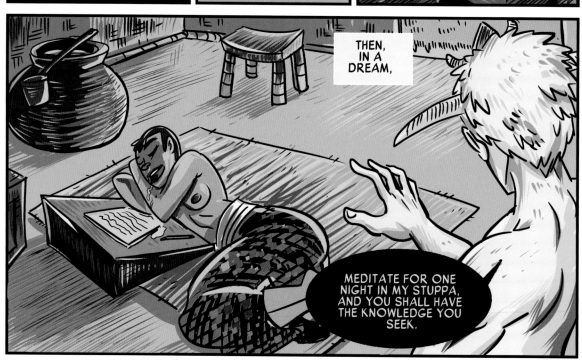

THEN, IN A DREAM,

MEDITATE FOR ONE NIGHT IN MY STUPPA, AND YOU SHALL HAVE THE KNOWLEDGE YOU SEEK.

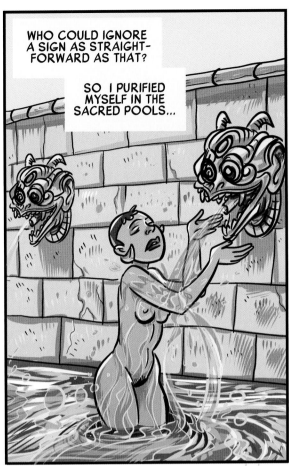

WHO COULD IGNORE A SIGN AS STRAIGHT-FORWARD AS THAT?

SO I PURIFIED MYSELF IN THE SACRED POOLS...

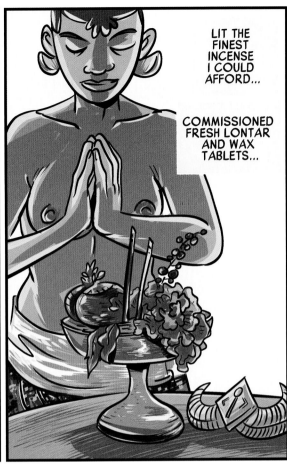

LIT THE FINEST INCENSE I COULD AFFORD...

COMMISSIONED FRESH LONTAR AND WAX TABLETS...

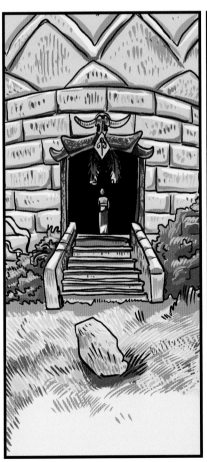

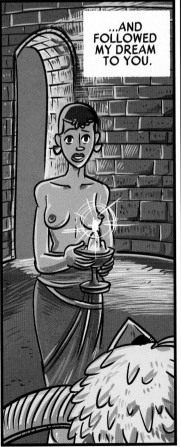

...AND FOLLOWED MY DREAM TO YOU.

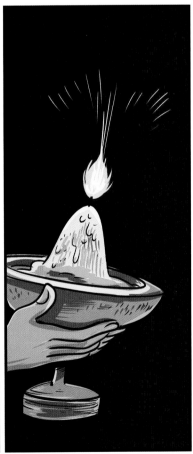

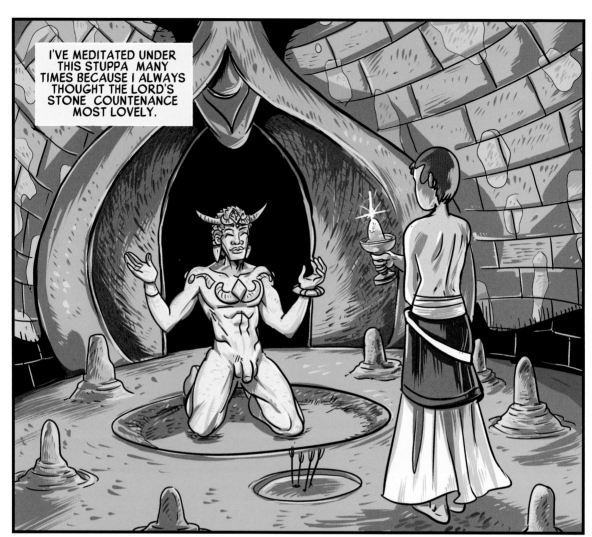

I'VE MEDITATED UNDER THIS STUPPA MANY TIMES BECAUSE I ALWAYS THOUGHT THE LORD'S STONE COUNTENANCE MOST LOVELY.

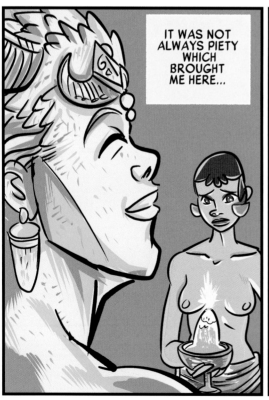

IT WAS NOT ALWAYS PIETY WHICH BROUGHT ME HERE...

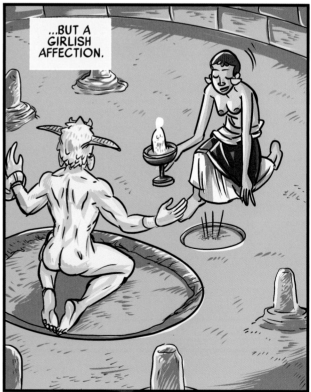

...BUT A GIRLISH AFFECTION.

184

WELL THEN...
LET'S BEGIN...
...HOW LONG HAS IT BEEN?
IT MUST BE APPROACHING THE BELLY OF THE NIGHT.
HMM?

WHAT-WHAT !?!

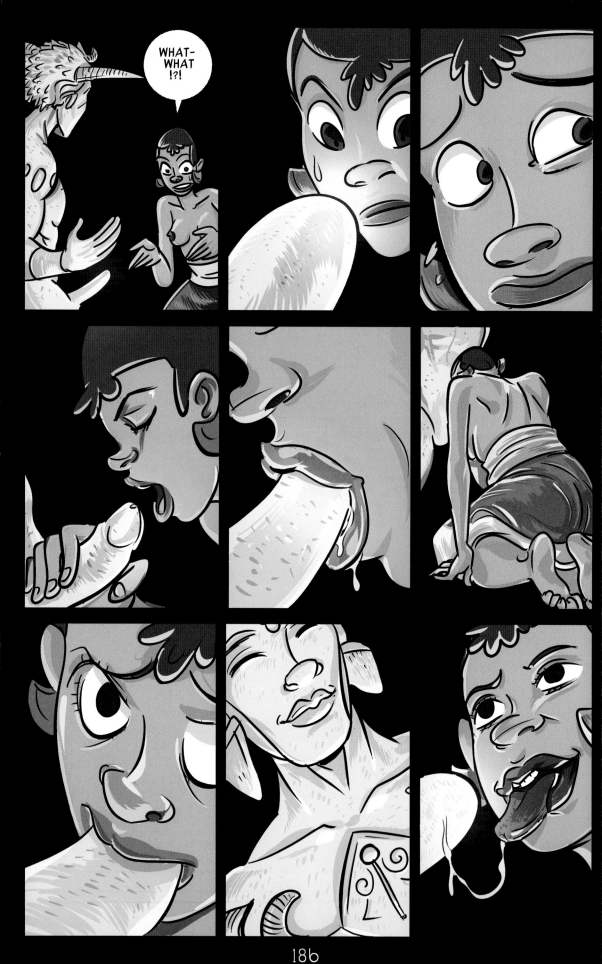

MY GOODNESS! I'VE ALWAYS WANTED TO DO THAT! BUT I CAN'T BELIEVE I ACTUALLY--
OH!
WET!
UHHHHHM...! S-SHOULD I...?

EITHER I'M INSANE, OR THE GOD' CALLS ME TO WAKE HIM.
GENTLY NOW...
I'M NOT SO YOUNG...
EASE IT IN SLOWLY...

IT FITS! IT SLID SO EASILY INSIDE!

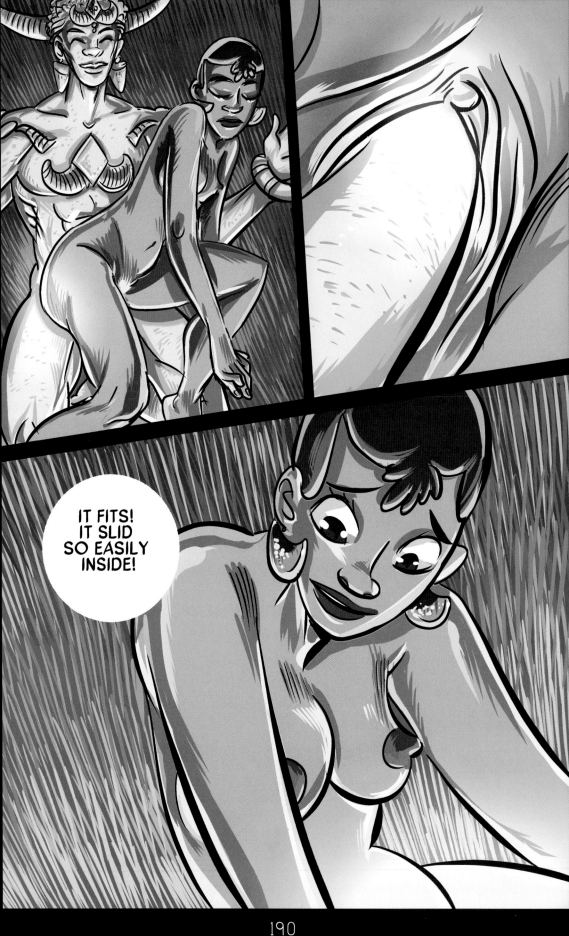

SO, WHAT NOW? SHOULD I ROCK FORWARD, OR...
WELL MET, MY DEAR WAJAT!
OH! AM I DREAMING?
DOES IT MATTER? DID YOU NOT ASK THIS OF ME?
I PRAYED FOR DIVINE INSPIRATION-!
THAT, YOUR BODY WILL PROVIDE. I AM MERELY ITS INSTRUMENT.
♥

HAHAHA-
HA

194

HOW WONDERFUL, SISTER WAJAT!!
A MOST STIMULATING AND LASCIVIOUS ...
...FIRST VERSE.
...FIRST!?!
I THINK A HYMN THIS EXCELLENT CAN BE DEVELOPED INTO AN ENTIRE EPIC, DON'T YOU THINK?
WE SHALL CARVE IT ON THE WALLS OF A NEW TEMPLE TO THE RED CHAMBER!
!

I...
I SUPPOSE I'LL HAVE TO MEDITATE MUCH MORE, THEN. AT LEAST ONCE PER VERSE.
DO WHAT YOU HAVE TO.

DID YOU KNOW... THERE ARE OVER A THOUSAND VERSES IN AN EPIC?

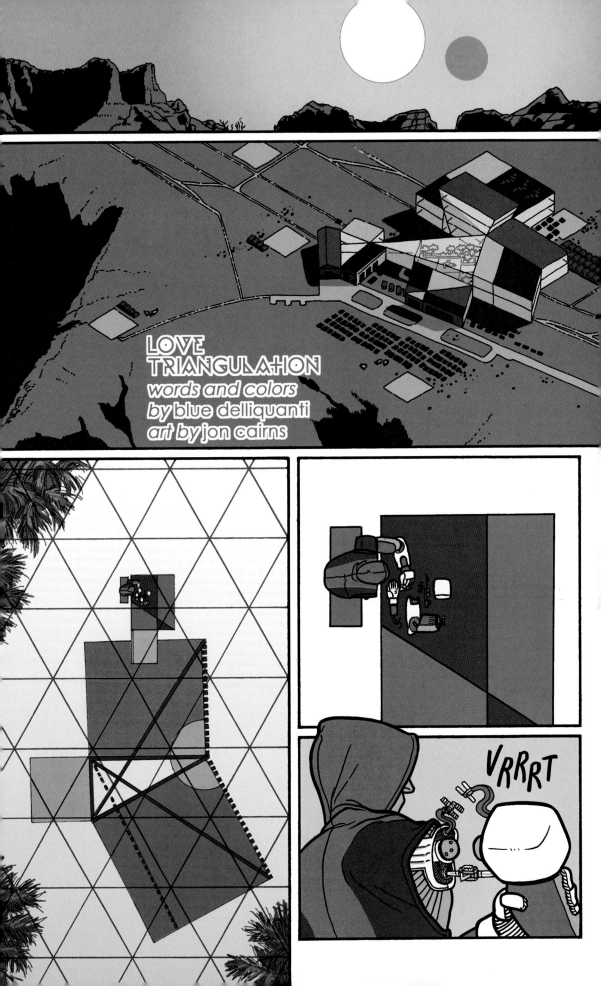

LOVE TRIANGULATION
*words and colors
by blue delliquanti
art by jon cairns*

VRRRT

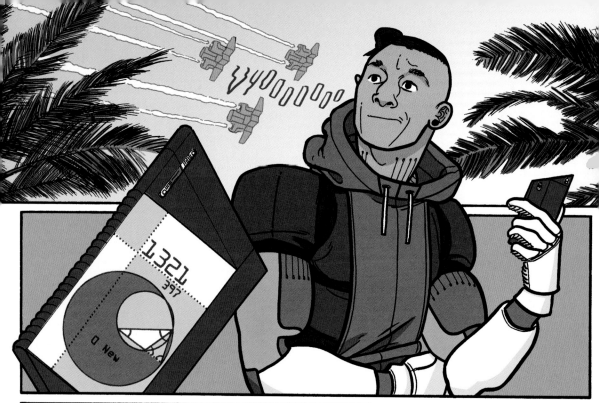

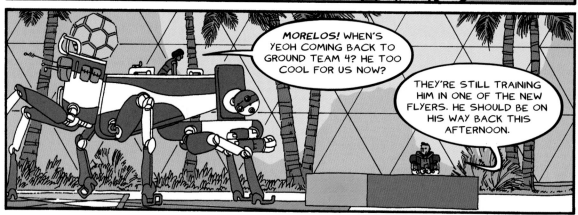

MORELOS! WHEN'S YEOH COMING BACK TO GROUND TEAM 4? HE TOO COOL FOR US NOW?

THEY'RE STILL TRAINING HIM IN ONE OF THE NEW FLYERS. HE SHOULD BE ON HIS WAY BACK THIS AFTERNOON.

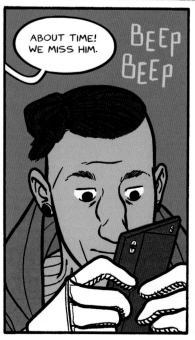

ABOUT TIME! WE MISS HIM.

BEEP BEEP

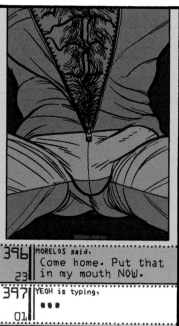

396
23
MORELOS said,
Come home. Put that in my mouth NOW.

397
01
YEOH is typing,
...

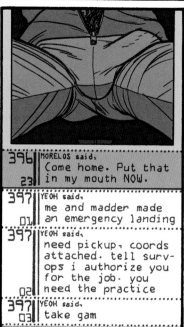

396
23
MORELOS said,
Come home. Put that in my mouth NOW.

397
01
YEOH said,
me and madder made an emergency landing

397
02
YEOH said,
need pickup, coords attached. tell surv-ops i authorize you for the job. you need the practice

397
03
YEOH said,
take gam

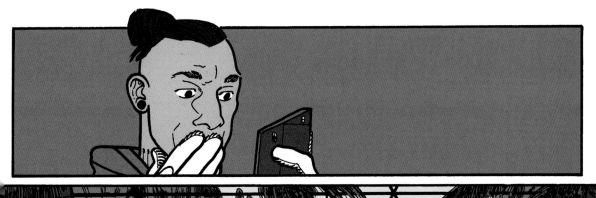

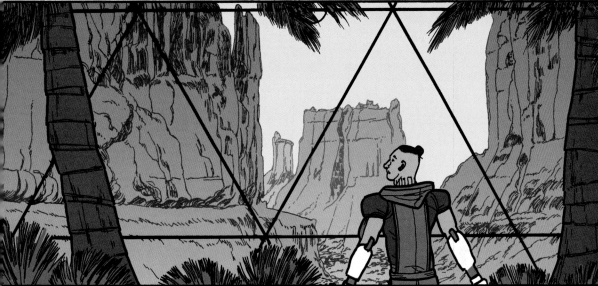

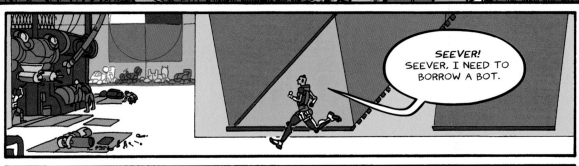

SEEVER! SEEVER, I NEED TO BORROW A BOT.

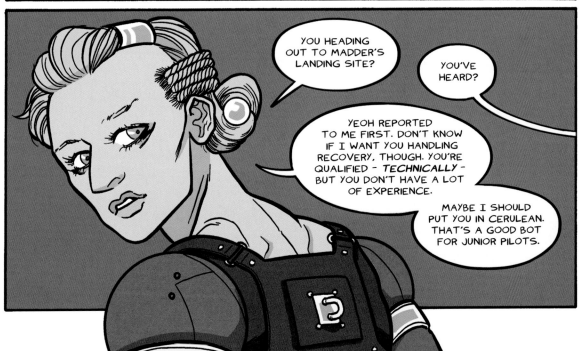

YOU HEADING OUT TO MADDER'S LANDING SITE?

YOU'VE HEARD?

YEOH REPORTED TO ME FIRST. DON'T KNOW IF I WANT YOU HANDLING RECOVERY, THOUGH. YOU'RE QUALIFIED — *TECHNICALLY* — BUT YOU DON'T HAVE A LOT OF EXPERIENCE.

MAYBE I SHOULD PUT YOU IN CERULEAN. THAT'S A GOOD BOT FOR JUNIOR PILOTS.

NO, I -
HE WANTS ME TO USE A SPECIFIC ONE.
"GAM," HE CALLED IT. I THINK HE USES THAT ONE A LOT - MAYBE I CAN HANDLE IT OKAY -
GAMBOGE?
I GUESS. IT IS YEOH'S FAVORITE. BUT YOU'D BETTER TREAT IT RIGHT.
GAM, YOU'RE UP FOR A MISSION.
YEOH? IS HE BACK?
OH, NO, I -
MY NAME IS MORELOS.
BUT I'M GOING OUT TO LOOK FOR YEOH. HE HAD A CRASH LANDING AND HE'S STRANDED OUT THERE.
YOU'VE WORKED WITH HIM BEFORE -
WILL YOU HELP ME?
IT'D BE MY PLEASURE.
YOU'RE WELCOME TO CLIMB INSIDE, MORELOS.

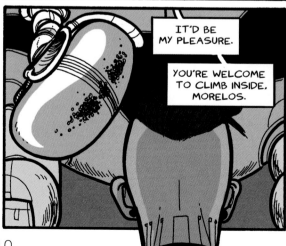

I'VE TRIANGULATED THE COORDINATES AND LOGGED THE RECOVERY PLAN. YOU CAN MOVE OUT AT ANY TIME.
YOU REMEMBER HOW TO INTERFACE WITH THESE GUYS, RIGHT?
OF COURSE! IT'S JUST . . . BEEN A WHILE.
YEOH MADE SOME CUSTOM MODIFICATIONS TO MY INTERFACE LINKS.
BUT I THINK THE CHANGES WILL HELP YOU FEEL MORE COMFORTABLE.
WELCOME ABOARD. WHEN YOU'RE READY, PLEASE ALIGN YOUR LIMBS ON THE MARKED POINTS AND I'LL FIRE UP THE INTERFACE.
VRRRT
VRRT

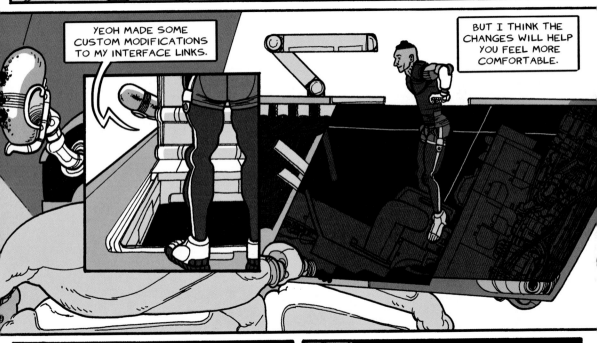

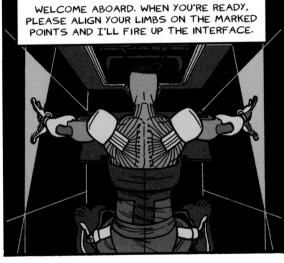

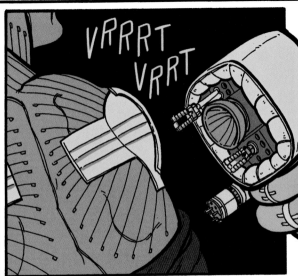

sst
Tss
Tss
sst
WHOA.
HOW WAS THAT?
NOT AS ROUGH AS OTHER LINKS I'VE DONE, BUT . . .
vrch
vrip vip
vip vir
riii
vrip
vrip
vrch
STILL TAKES GETTING USED TO.
NO PROBLEM. WE'LL TAKE IT EASY AT FIRST.
TRY MANIPULATING MY FINE MOTOR APPENDAGES AS IF THEY WERE YOUR OWN ARMS.
Wirr
EXCELLENT! WE'LL DO FINE. LET'S FIND YEOH'S SHIP AND BRING HIM AND THE SHIP'S AI BACK TO BASE.

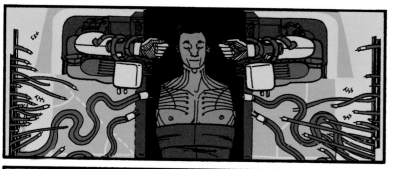

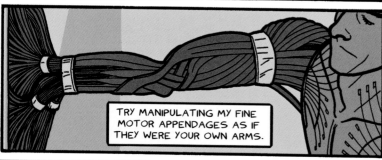

clack

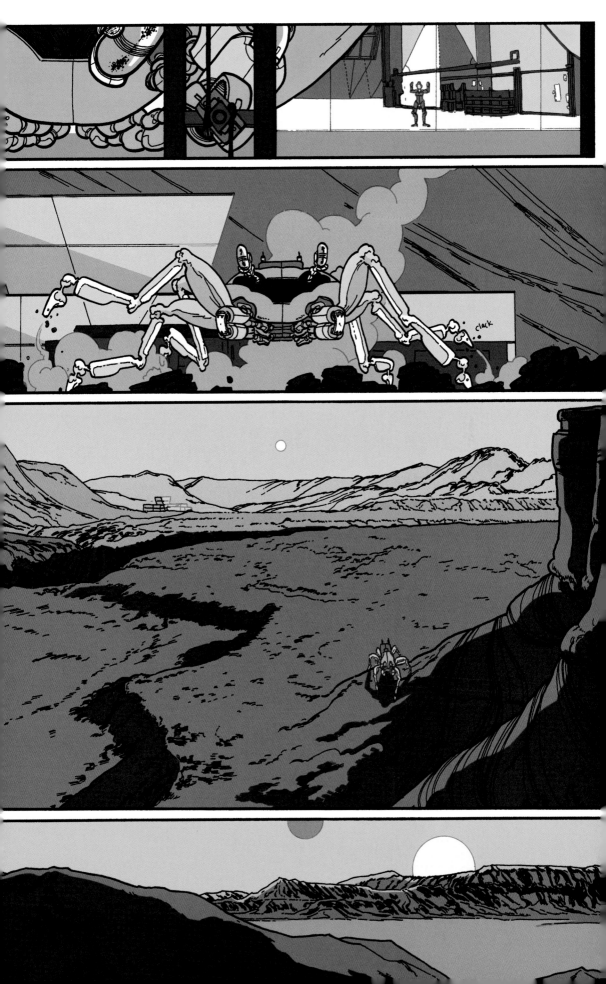

SO, GAMBOGE -
OH, YOU CAN CALL ME GAM.
GAM.
YEOH'S PILOTED YOU FOR A FEW YEARS, HASN'T HE? I'VE HEARD HIM MENTION YOU. MAYBE SHOWN ME A PICTURE.
YES, HE'S BEEN MY PRIMARY PILOT FOR ALMOST 3 YEARS. OUR SURVEY RADIUS ON THE SOUTHERN CONTINENT IS ALMOST 700 KILOMETERS WIDE.
SKLIK
KLAK
KRUMP
KRAK
GAM -!
ONE MOMENT, CORRECTING -
KRAK
KRAK
SKRIK
KRAK
KLANG

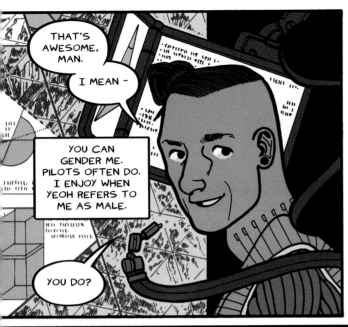

THAT'S AWESOME, MAN.

I MEAN –

YOU CAN GENDER ME. PILOTS OFTEN DO. I ENJOY WHEN YEOH REFERS TO ME AS MALE.

YOU DO?

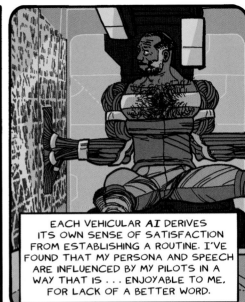

EACH VEHICULAR *AI* DERIVES ITS OWN SENSE OF SATISFACTION FROM ESTABLISHING A ROUTINE. I'VE FOUND THAT MY PERSONA AND SPEECH ARE INFLUENCED BY MY PILOTS IN A WAY THAT IS . . . ENJOYABLE TO ME, FOR LACK OF A BETTER WORD.

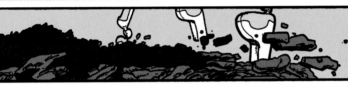

HAHA. LISTEN, BUDDY, THERE'S NOTHING WRONG WITH HAVING A ROUTINE.

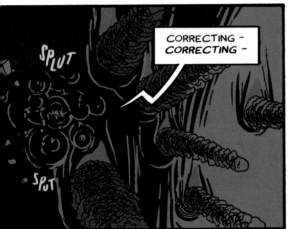

SPLUT

SPUT

CORRECTING – CORRECTING –

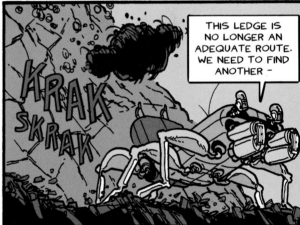

KRAK SKRAK

THIS LEDGE IS NO LONGER AN ADEQUATE ROUTE. WE NEED TO FIND ANOTHER –

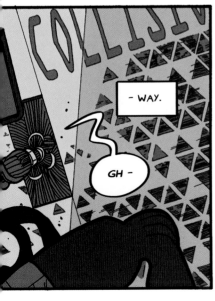

COLLISI

– WAY.

GH –

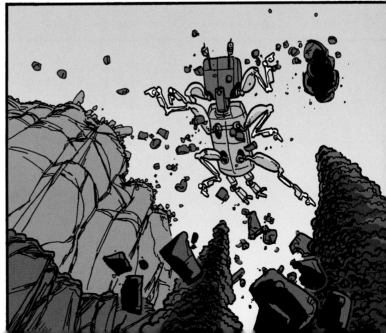

GRIIICH
MORELOS, WAIT -
I'M NOT DESIGNED TO CLIMB THIS WAY -
GRIIICH
I AM. PLEASE. TRUST ME WITH THE CLIMBING. YOU FIGURE OUT OUR EXIT.
ROTATE 76 DEGREES CLOCKWISE AROUND THE TRUNK, AND CLIMB 5 METERS. KICK OFF WHEN I SAY SO.
NOW.
GRICH
GRICH
CRASH

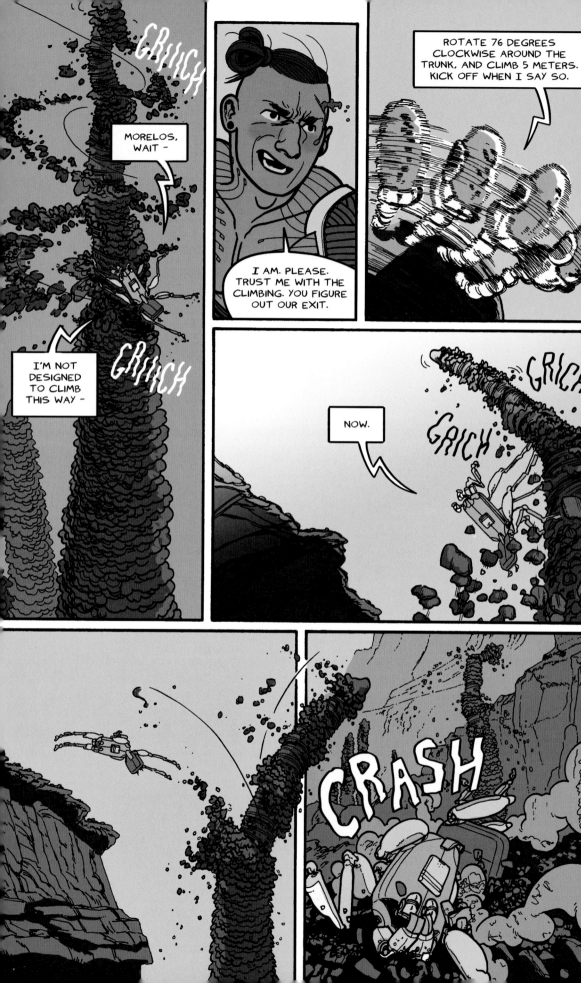

GOT IT!
GAM, CAN I TAKE US ALONG THIS LEDGE?
CONFIRMED. THIS ROUTE IS VIABLE. WELL DONE, MORELOS.
LOOKS LIKE YOU COULD USE A HAND WITH THAT INJURY. MAY I BORROW YOURS?
HUH? SURE, I MEAN -
- OH.
YOU CAN REMAIN LINKED THIS WAY. I'LL ONLY TAKE A SECOND.
IS THIS ONE OF YEOH'S BIG MODIFICATIONS?
WE BOTH HAD A SAY IN IT. IT HELPS TO BE ABLE TO CARE FOR MY PILOT WHILE HE'S HANDLING MY NAVIGATION.
HEH. I CAN IMAGINE.
YOU AND YEOH ARE BOTH PRETTY SMART.
DON'T SELL YOURSELF SHORT.

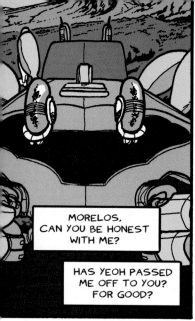

MORELOS, CAN YOU BE HONEST WITH ME?

HAS YEOH PASSED ME OFF TO YOU? FOR GOOD?

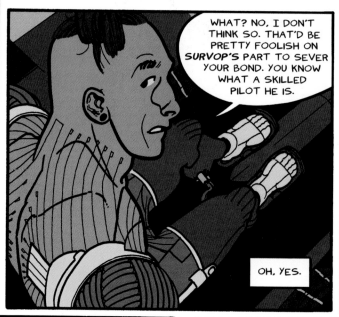

WHAT? NO, I DON'T THINK SO. THAT'D BE PRETTY FOOLISH ON *SURVOP'S* PART TO SEVER YOUR BOND. YOU KNOW WHAT A SKILLED PILOT HE IS.

OH, YES.

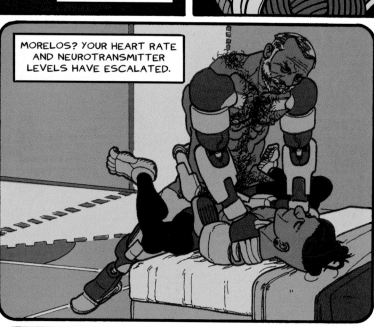

MORELOS? YOUR HEART RATE AND NEUROTRANSMITTER LEVELS HAVE ESCALATED.

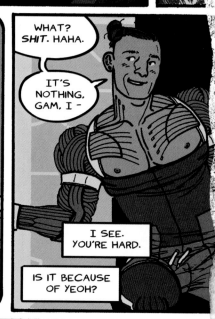

WHAT? *SHIT.* HAHA.

IT'S NOTHING, GAM, I —

I SEE. YOU'RE HARD.

IS IT BECAUSE OF YEOH?

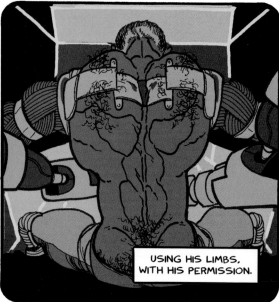

USING HIS LIMBS, WITH HIS PERMISSION.

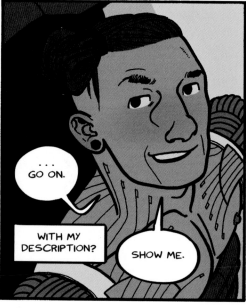

. . . GO ON.

WITH MY DESCRIPTION?

SHOW ME.

208

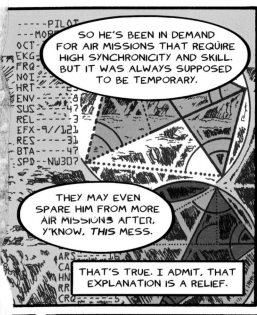

SO HE'S BEEN IN DEMAND FOR AIR MISSIONS THAT REQUIRE HIGH SYNCHRONICITY AND SKILL. BUT IT WAS ALWAYS SUPPOSED TO BE TEMPORARY.

THEY MAY EVEN SPARE HIM FROM MORE AIR MISSIONS AFTER, Y'KNOW, *THIS* MESS.

THAT'S TRUE. I ADMIT, THAT EXPLANATION IS A RELIEF.

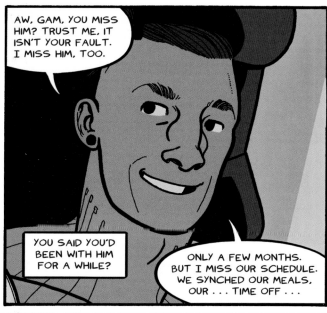

AW, GAM, YOU MISS HIM? TRUST ME, IT ISN'T YOUR FAULT. I MISS HIM, TOO.

YOU SAID YOU'D BEEN WITH HIM FOR A WHILE?

ONLY A FEW MONTHS. BUT I MISS OUR SCHEDULE. WE SYNCHED OUR MEALS, OUR . . . TIME OFF . . .

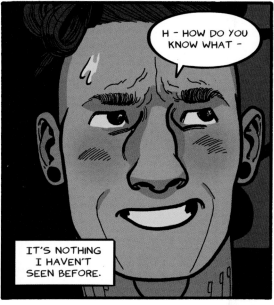

H - HOW DO YOU KNOW WHAT -

IT'S NOTHING I HAVEN'T SEEN BEFORE.

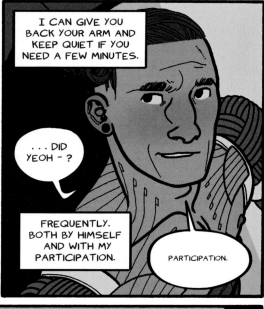

I CAN GIVE YOU BACK YOUR ARM AND KEEP QUIET IF YOU NEED A FEW MINUTES.

. . . DID YEOH - ?

FREQUENTLY. BOTH BY HIMSELF AND WITH MY PARTICIPATION.

PARTICIPATION.

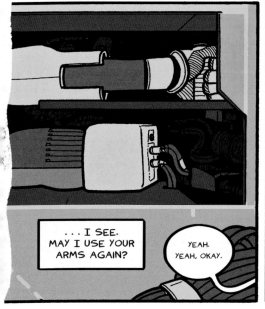

. . . I SEE. MAY I USE YOUR ARMS AGAIN?

YEAH. YEAH, OKAY.

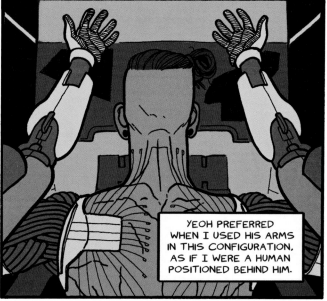

YEOH PREFERRED WHEN I USED HIS ARMS IN THIS CONFIGURATION, AS IF I WERE A HUMAN POSITIONED BEHIND HIM.

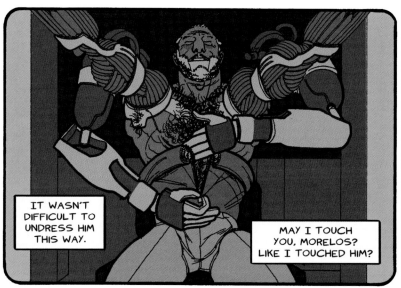

IT WASN'T DIFFICULT TO UNDRESS HIM THIS WAY.

MAY I TOUCH YOU, MORELOS? LIKE I TOUCHED HIM?

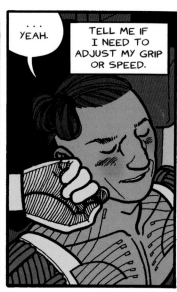

. . . YEAH.

TELL ME IF I NEED TO ADJUST MY GRIP OR SPEED.

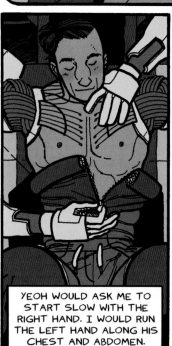

YEOH WOULD ASK ME TO START SLOW WITH THE RIGHT HAND. I WOULD RUN THE LEFT HAND ALONG HIS CHEST AND ABDOMEN.

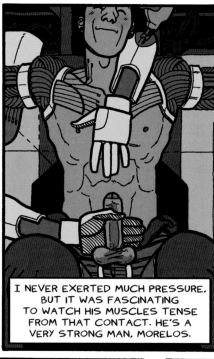

I NEVER EXERTED MUCH PRESSURE, BUT IT WAS FASCINATING TO WATCH HIS MUSCLES TENSE FROM THAT CONTACT. HE'S A VERY STRONG MAN, MORELOS.

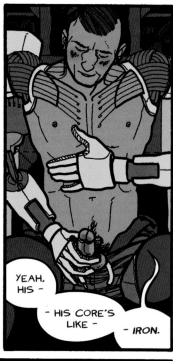

YEAH, HIS —

— HIS CORE'S LIKE —

— IRON.

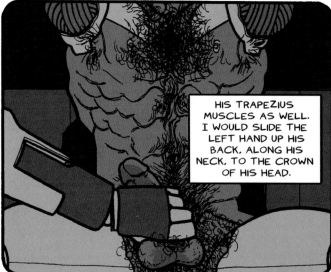

HIS TRAPEZIUS MUSCLES AS WELL. I WOULD SLIDE THE LEFT HAND UP HIS BACK, ALONG HIS NECK, TO THE CROWN OF HIS HEAD.

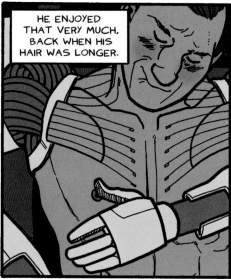

HE ENJOYED THAT VERY MUCH, BACK WHEN HIS HAIR WAS LONGER.

YOU'RE BUCKING INTO MY GRIP. SHOULD I GO FASTER -
YES.
YOU HAVE SO MUCH HAIR, MORELOS. DOES YEOH ENJOY RUNNING HIS HANDS THROUGH IT, TOO? MAY I -
PLEASE.
UNH -
DID YOU -
HAVE YOU FUCKED HIM?
YOU MEAN WITH - ?
SOMETIMES WHEN I SUCK HIS COCK HE LETS ME FINGER HIM.
HE LOOKS SO GOOD, GAM. HAVE YOU SEEN WHAT HE'S LIKE WHEN HE'S GETTING FUCKED?
. . .
I HAVE.
SHOW ME. TELL ME HOW YOU'VE DONE IT.
MORELOS, I -
THIS IS JUST YOUR FIRST TIME WITH ME. I DON'T WANT TO MISJUDGE MY STRENGTH AND HURT YOU -
YOU WON'T, GAM. PLEASE.
FUCK ME.

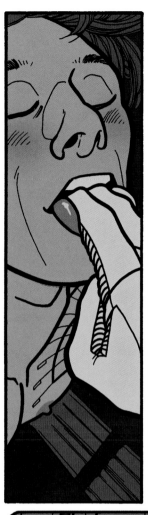

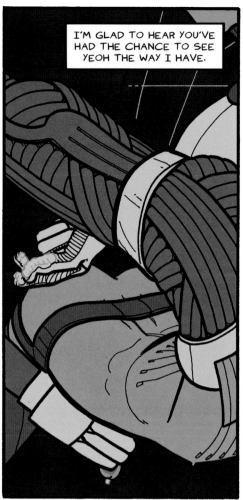

I'M GLAD TO HEAR YOU'VE HAD THE CHANCE TO SEE YEOH THE WAY I HAVE.

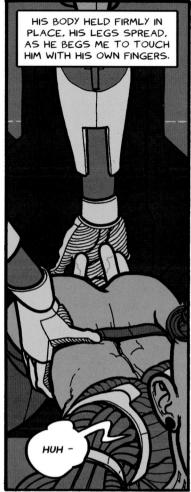

HIS BODY HELD FIRMLY IN PLACE, HIS LEGS SPREAD, AS HE BEGS ME TO TOUCH HIM WITH HIS OWN FINGERS.

HUH –

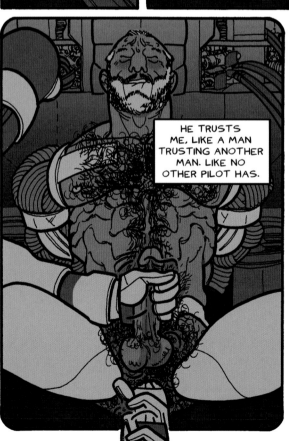

HE TRUSTS ME, LIKE A MAN TRUSTING ANOTHER MAN. LIKE NO OTHER PILOT HAS.

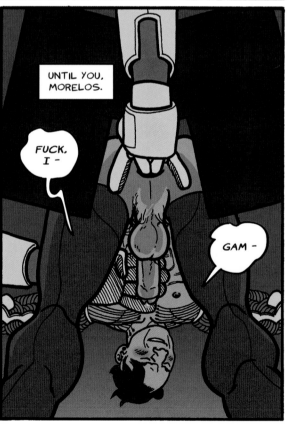

UNTIL YOU, MORELOS.

FUCK, I –

GAM –

212

!
AH –
HHH –
I UNDERSTAND WHY YOU ARE SO FOND OF HIM.
I SHARE THE SAME FONDNESS FOR MY FAVORITE PILOTS.

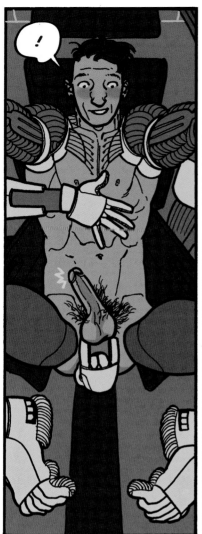

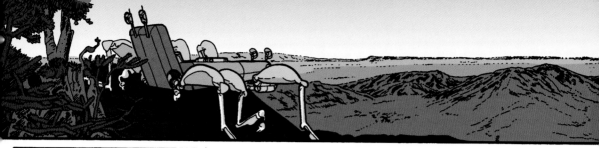

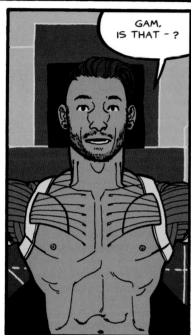

GAM, IS THAT -?

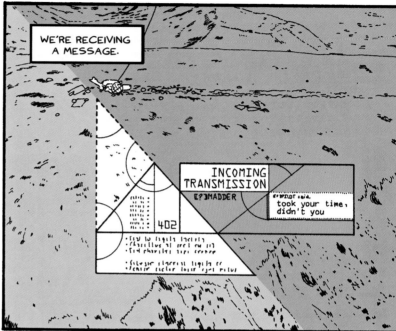

WE'RE RECEIVING A MESSAGE.

INCOMING TRANSMISSION

[?]MADDER

took your time, didn't you

402

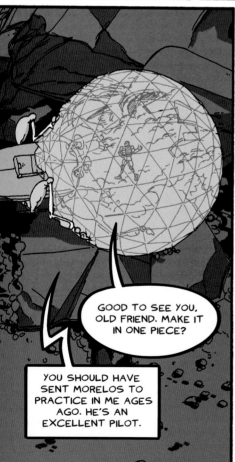

GOOD TO SEE YOU, OLD FRIEND. MAKE IT IN ONE PIECE?

YOU SHOULD HAVE SENT MORELOS TO PRACTICE IN ME AGES AGO. HE'S AN EXCELLENT PILOT.

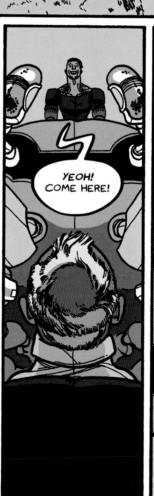

YEOH! COME HERE!

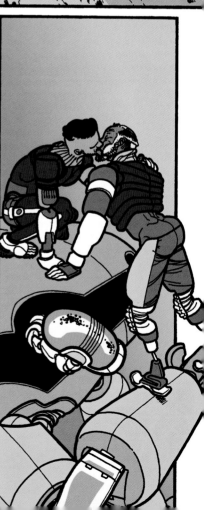

FIRST THINGS FIRST.
OF COURSE. I DETACHED MADDER'S AI CORE TO TAKE BACK WITH US. SHE'S FINE, JUST TAKING A NAP AFTER -
HOW LONG HAVE YOU BEEN FUCKING YOUR ROBOT TANK, YEOH?
WHY HAVEN'T YOU TOLD ME HOW GOOD GAM IS?
I KEPT TELLING YOU THAT YOU NEEDED MORE PRACTICE IN THE BOTS.
I FOR ONE, YEOH, WOULD APPRECIATE THE COMPANY WHILE YOU'RE TEMPORARILY REASSIGNED.

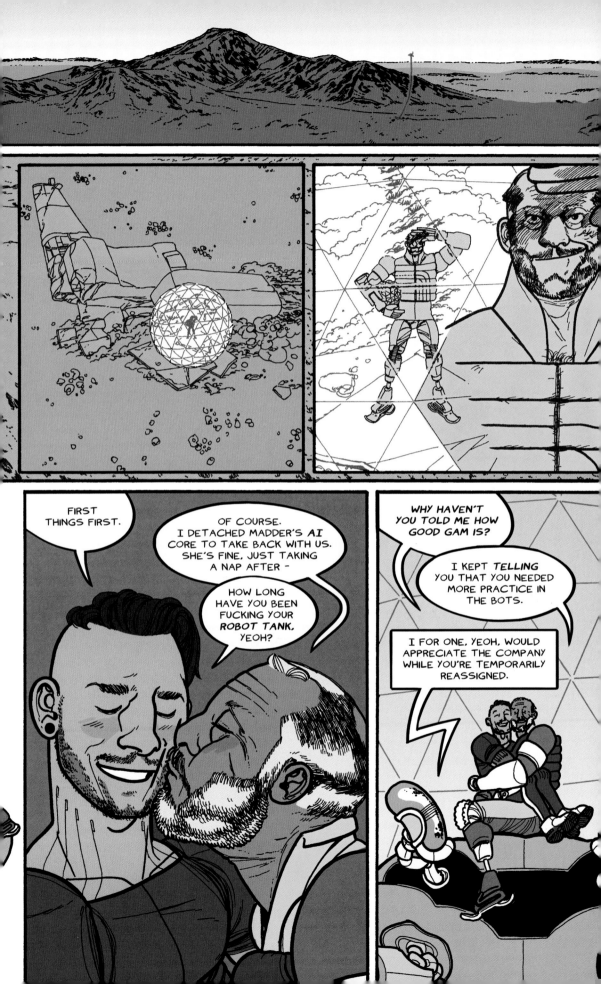

GAM'S RIGHT OF COURSE. I SHOULD TREAT MY BOYS BETTER, ESPECIALLY IF THEY'RE GOING TO HAVE FUN WITHOUT ME.
WE BOTH MISSED YOU, YEOH.
SHALL WE GET GOING?
WHO'S GOING TO LINK UP?
YOU, OF COURSE. I WANT TO SEE THE MASTER PILOT AT WORK.
NOT TO MENTION GAM DESCRIBED SOME THINGS I WANT TO SEE FOR MYSELF.
OH, YES.
THERE'S NOTHING QUITE LIKE WORKING WITH MY PILOTS.
THE END

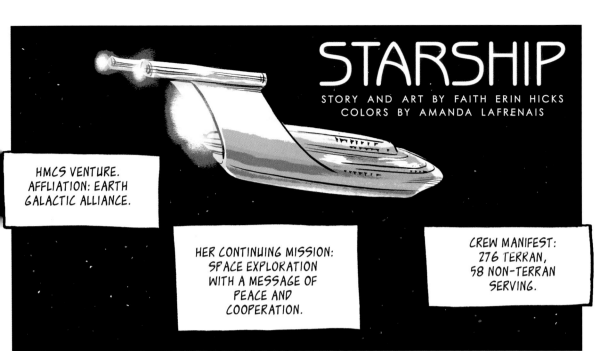

STARSHIP

STORY AND ART BY FAITH ERIN HICKS
COLORS BY AMANDA LAFRENAIS

HMCS VENTURE. AFFLIATION: EARTH GALACTIC ALLIANCE.

HER CONTINUING MISSION: SPACE EXPLORATION WITH A MESSAGE OF PEACE AND COOPERATION.

CREW MANIFEST: 276 TERRAN, 58 NON-TERRAN SERVING.

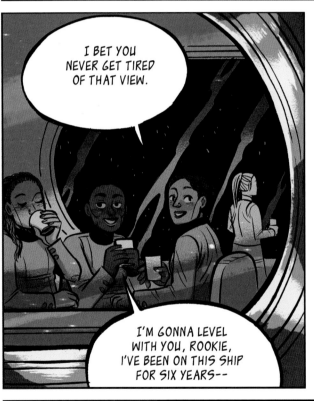

I BET YOU NEVER GET TIRED OF THAT VIEW.

I'M GONNA LEVEL WITH YOU, ROOKIE, I'VE BEEN ON THIS SHIP FOR SIX YEARS--

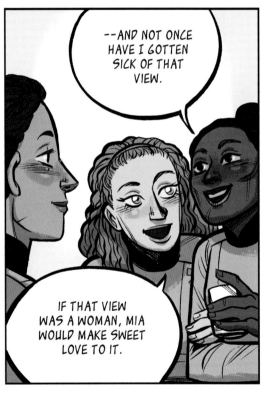

--AND NOT ONCE HAVE I GOTTEN SICK OF THAT VIEW.

IF THAT VIEW WAS A WOMAN, MIA WOULD MAKE SWEET LOVE TO IT.

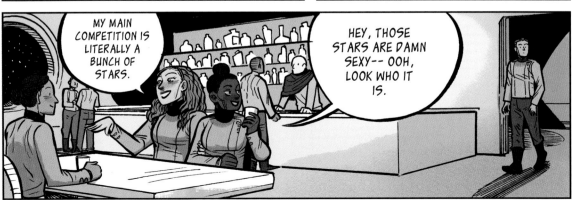

MY MAIN COMPETITION IS LITERALLY A BUNCH OF STARS.

HEY, THOSE STARS ARE DAMN SEXY-- OOH, LOOK WHO IT IS.

WHO'S THAT? IS HE NON-TERRAN?
THAT, ROOKIE, IS OUR VERY FIRST ANDROID CREWMEMBER.
YOU'RE KIDDING. FOR REAL?
YUP. HE WENT THROUGH THE GALACTIC ACADEMY AND EVERYTHING. THE CAPTAIN SAID WE WERE LUCKY TO GET HIM. TIN MAN KNOWS HIS ENGINES.
DON'T CALL HIM "TIN MAN," MIA. THAT'S RUDE. HE'S OUR CREWMATE.
SORRY, FEE, I KNOW YOU'RE ALL ABOUT THE ROBOT RIGHTS.
MIA, I LOVE YOU, BUT YOU'RE EMBARRASSING YOURSELF.
HE'S ... KIND OF BEAUTIFUL.

HEEYYY! ROOKIE LIKES THE TASTE OF METAL!
MIA, OH MY GOD.
UM, NOT LIKE THAT!
C'MON, FEE. I'M AN ASSHOLE, BUT I'M YOUR ASSHOLE, RIGHT?
UGGH! YOU'RE SO ANNOYING!
AND YOU LOVE MY ANNOYING ASS, DON'T YOU?
YEAH, OKAY. I LOVE YOUR ANNOYING ASS.

AHG! CRAP!

BZZT

YOU SON OF A ... CRAP.

EXCUSE ME.

CHIEF IRA SENT ME FOR AN UPDATE ON WHEN THE CONSOLE REPAIRS WOULD BE FINISHED.

IT'S ANYONE'S GUESS AT THIS POINT. YOU DON'T HAPPEN TO KNOW ANYTHING ABOUT 1801-D CHARGING PORTS, DO YOU?

I HAVE SOME KNOWLEDGE. WHAT'S THE ISSUE?

THIS DAMN CONSOLE KEEPS OVERCHARGING THE FIFTH DECK REPLICATORS. I'VE NO IDEA WHY.

BEEN WORKING ON IT FOR TWO HOURS. IT'S SO FRUSTRATING, I THOUGHT I COULD FIX ANYTHING.

IT MIGHT BE A CASCADE FAILURE. THE OLDER MODEL OF THIS CONSOLE IS KNOWN TO BE FAULTY. I'LL TAKE A LOOK.

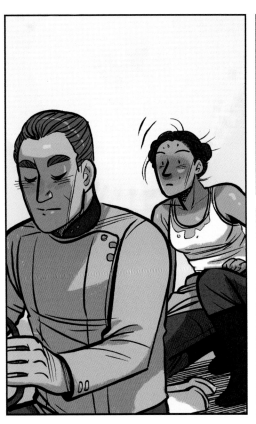

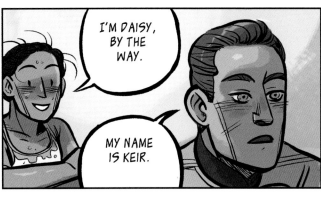

I'M DAISY, BY THE WAY.

MY NAME IS KEIR.

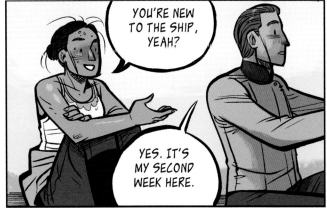

YOU'RE NEW TO THE SHIP, YEAH?

YES. IT'S MY SECOND WEEK HERE.

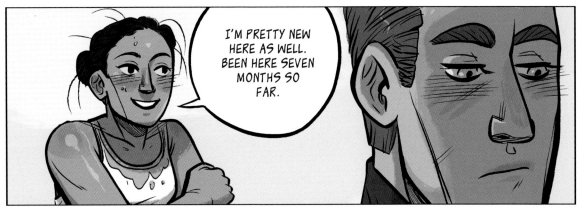

I'M PRETTY NEW HERE AS WELL. BEEN HERE SEVEN MONTHS SO FAR.

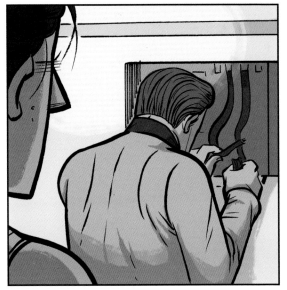

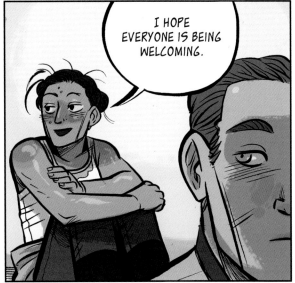

I HOPE EVERYONE IS BEING WELCOMING.

EVERYONE HAS BEEN VERY CORDIAL.

GOOD, I'M GLAD.

MAYBE IT'S NAIVE OF ME, BUT WHENEVER I LOOK OUT OF ONE OF VENTURE'S WINDOWS, I CAN FEEL HOW SMALL WE ARE IN THE GALAXY.

HUNDREDS OF PEOPLE ON THIS SHIP, A TINY SPECK OF WARMTH IN THE MIDST OF COLD VACUUM.

SO I ALWAYS HOPE THE PEOPLE I GET TO EXPLORE THE GALAXY WITH ARE ... *KIND*.

BECAUSE WE'RE ALL WE'VE GOT OUT HERE, YOU KNOW?
KLAK
THIS WIRE WAS IMPROPERLY THREADED, SO THAT WAS CAUSING THE MALFUNCTION.
OH MY GOD, DAISY, YOU ARE SUCH A DORK.

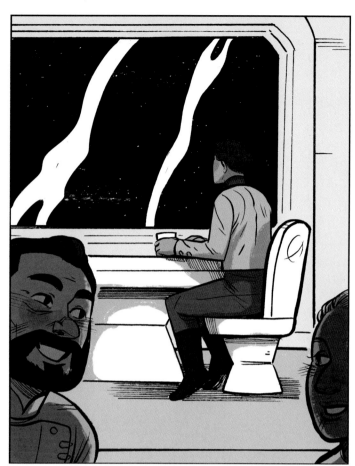

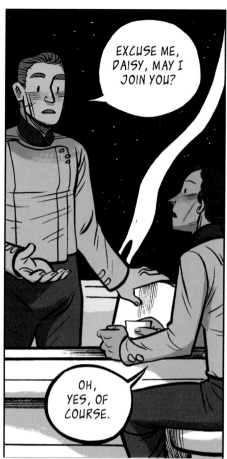

EXCUSE ME, DAISY, MAY I JOIN YOU?

OH, YES, OF COURSE.

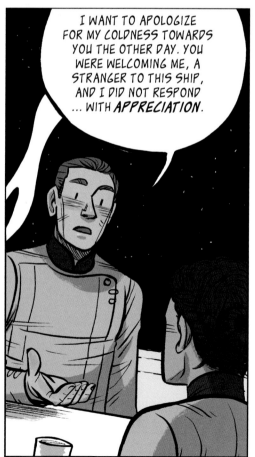

I WANT TO APOLOGIZE FOR MY COLDNESS TOWARDS YOU THE OTHER DAY. YOU WERE WELCOMING ME, A STRANGER TO THIS SHIP, AND I DID NOT RESPOND ... WITH *APPRECIATION*.

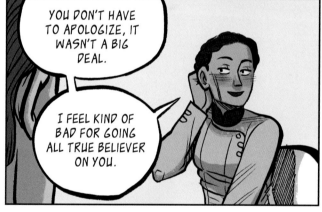

YOU DON'T HAVE TO APOLOGIZE, IT WASN'T A BIG DEAL.

I FEEL KIND OF BAD FOR GOING ALL TRUE BELIEVER ON YOU.

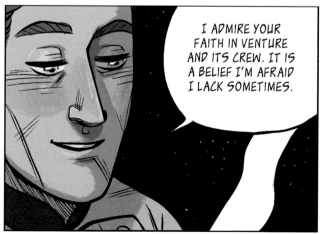

I ADMIRE YOUR FAITH IN VENTURE AND ITS CREW. IT IS A BELIEF I'M AFRAID I LACK SOMETIMES.

YOU DON'T BELIEVE IN OUR MISSION?
SPACE EXPLORATION UNDER A BANNER OF PEACE AND COOPERATION IS A WORTHY ENDEAVOR. I SUPPORT IT.
BUT YOU DON'T **BELIEVE** IN IT, RIGHT?
I'M AFRAID MY REASONS FOR PURSUING A CAREER ON THIS SHIP ARE MORE ... **PERSONAL**.
BY "PERSONAL" DO YOU MEAN SELFISH?
YES. THAT WAS VERY ASTUTE.
A SELFISH ANDROID. HOW WONDERFUL.

I'M SORRY, THAT WAS RUDE.
NO NEED TO APOLOGIZE.
I'M FLATTERED YOU FIND ME WONDERFUL.
SO WHAT'S YOUR SELFISH REASON FOR BEING ON THIS SHIP?
I'M AFRAID I DON'T KNOW YOU WELL ENOUGH TO TELL YOU THAT.
FAIR ENOUGH.
BUT KEIR, HERE'S THE SECRET: **EVERYONE** ON THIS SHIP IS HERE FOR SELFISH REASONS.
CHIEF ENGINEER IRA WANTS HIS NAME IN HISTORY BOOKS. THE MAN WHO'S REACHED THE FARTHEST CORNER OF EXPLORED SPACE.

I KNOW ONE CREW MEMBER WHO WANTS A POLITICAL CAREER, AND BEING A SPACE HERO IS A HELL OF A BOOST FOR THAT.
I KNOW SOMEONE ELSE WHO FOLLOWED HER GIRLFRIEND HERE.
EVERYONE ON THIS SHIP IS SELFISH, WHETHER THEY CHOOSE TO ADMIT IT OR NOT.
EVEN YOU?
EVEN ME.
WHAT'S YOUR SELFISH REASON FOR BEING ON THIS SHIP?
I'M AFRAID I DON'T KNOW YOU WELL ENOUGH TO TELL YOU THAT.
UNLESS YOU WANT TO COME BACK TO MY ROOM... AND GET TO KNOW ME BETTER.

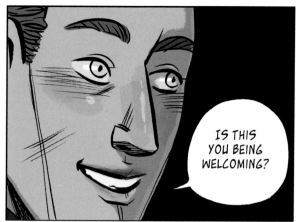

IS THIS YOU BEING WELCOMING?

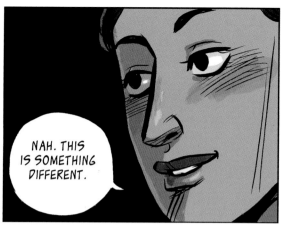

NAH. THIS IS SOMETHING DIFFERENT.

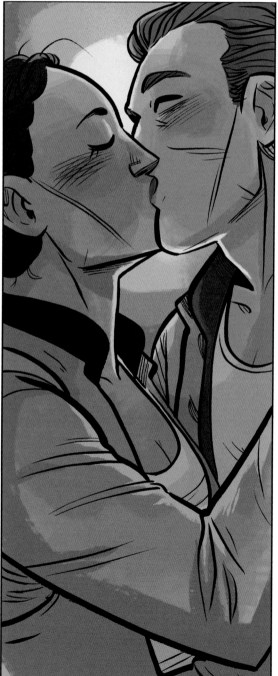

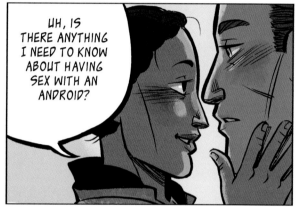

UH, IS THERE ANYTHING I NEED TO KNOW ABOUT HAVING SEX WITH AN ANDROID?

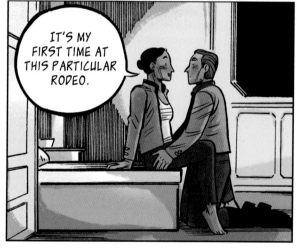

IT'S MY FIRST TIME AT THIS PARTICULAR RODEO.

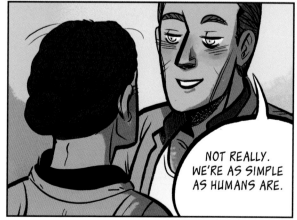

NOT REALLY. WE'RE AS SIMPLE AS HUMANS ARE.

YOU REALLY THINK HUMANS ARE SIMPLE?
SOMETIMES.
HAHH
AAHH

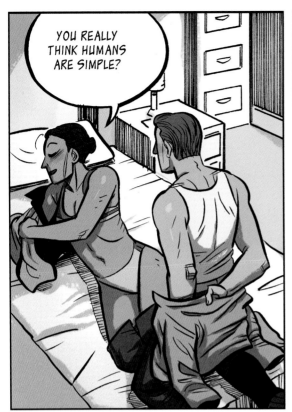

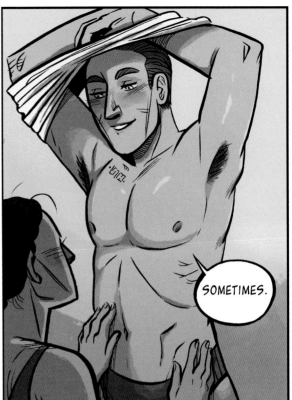

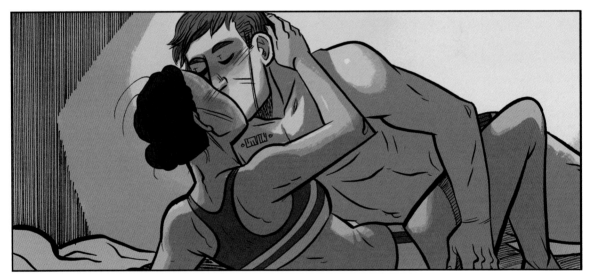

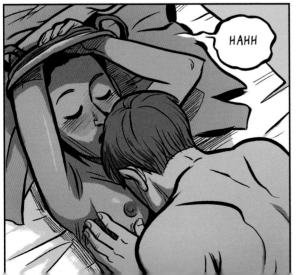

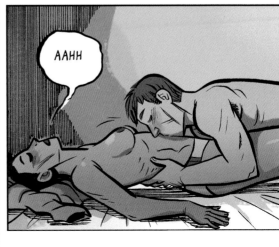

AAHH YAAYY

AHH!

HAH

UHN

HAAH
UHN!

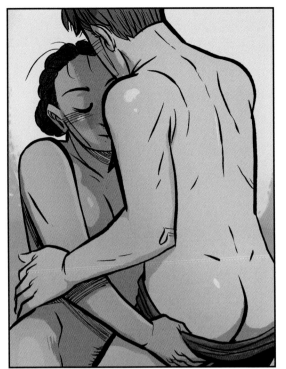

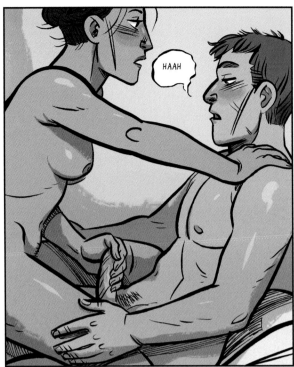

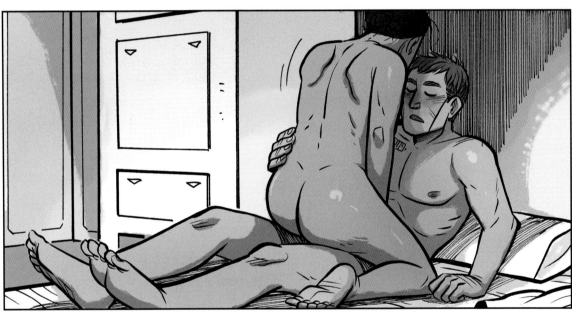

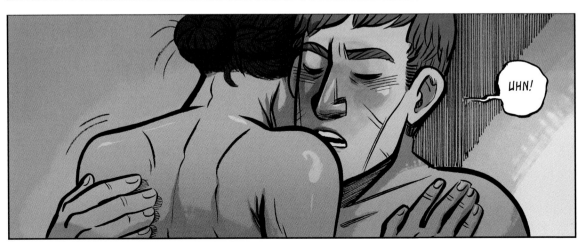

AH! AH! AH! AH! AH! AH! AH! AHHHH♡

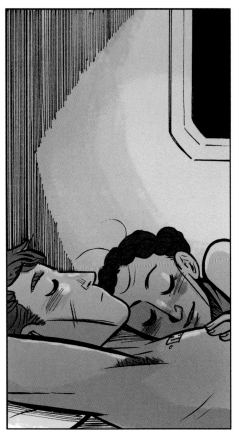

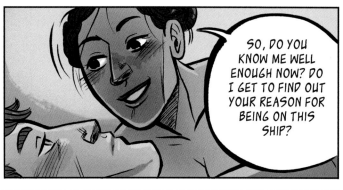

SO, DO YOU KNOW ME WELL ENOUGH NOW? DO I GET TO FIND OUT YOUR REASON FOR BEING ON THIS SHIP?

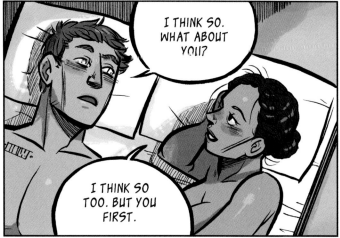

I THINK SO. WHAT ABOUT YOU?

I THINK SO TOO. BUT YOU FIRST.

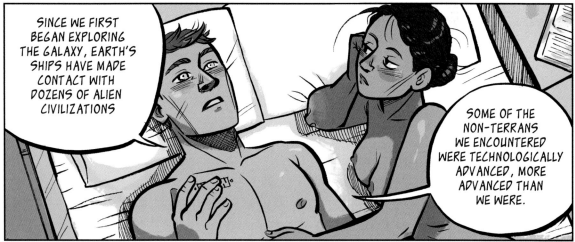

SINCE WE FIRST BEGAN EXPLORING THE GALAXY, EARTH'S SHIPS HAVE MADE CONTACT WITH DOZENS OF ALIEN CIVILIZATIONS

SOME OF THE NON-TERRANS WE ENCOUNTERED WERE TECHNOLOGICALLY ADVANCED, MORE ADVANCED THAN WE WERE.

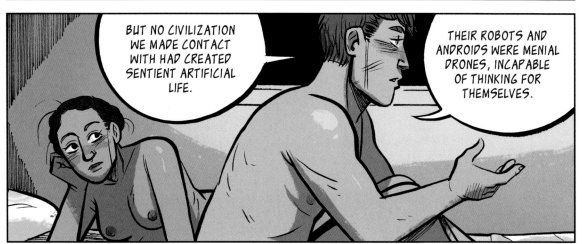

BUT NO CIVILIZATION WE MADE CONTACT WITH HAD CREATED SENTIENT ARTIFICIAL LIFE.

THEIR ROBOTS AND ANDROIDS WERE MENIAL DRONES, INCAPABLE OF THINKING FOR THEMSELVES.

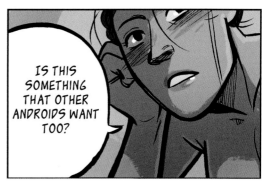

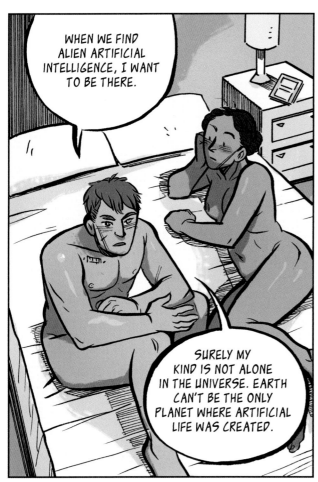

WHEN WE FIND ALIEN ARTIFICIAL INTELLIGENCE, I WANT TO BE THERE.

IS THIS SOMETHING THAT OTHER ANDROIDS WANT TOO?

SURELY MY KIND IS NOT ALONE IN THE UNIVERSE. EARTH CAN'T BE THE ONLY PLANET WHERE ARTIFICIAL LIFE WAS CREATED.

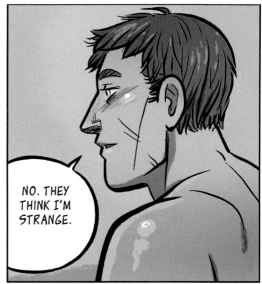

NO. THEY THINK I'M STRANGE.

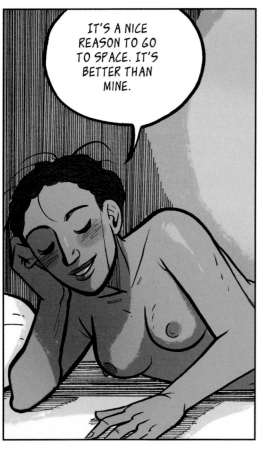

IT'S A NICE REASON TO GO TO SPACE. IT'S BETTER THAN MINE.

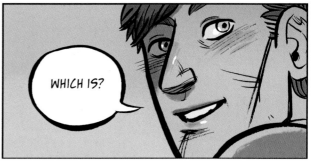

WHICH IS?

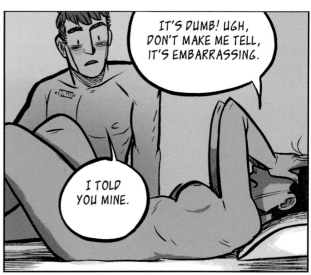

IT'S DUMB! UGH, DON'T MAKE ME TELL, IT'S EMBARRASSING.

I TOLD YOU MINE.

234

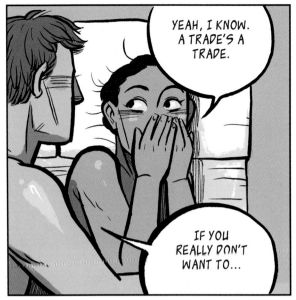

YEAH, I KNOW. A TRADE'S A TRADE.

IF YOU REALLY DON'T WANT TO...

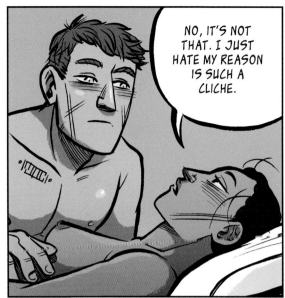

NO, IT'S NOT THAT. I JUST HATE MY REASON IS SUCH A CLICHE.

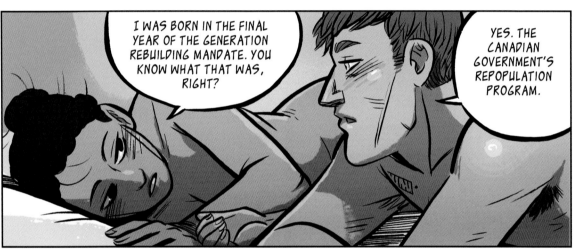

I WAS BORN IN THE FINAL YEAR OF THE GENERATION REBUILDING MANDATE. YOU KNOW WHAT THAT WAS, RIGHT?

YES. THE CANADIAN GOVERNMENT'S REPOPULATION PROGRAM.

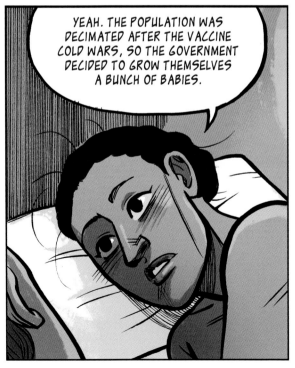

YEAH. THE POPULATION WAS DECIMATED AFTER THE VACCINE COLD WARS, SO THE GOVERNMENT DECIDED TO GROW THEMSELVES A BUNCH OF BABIES.

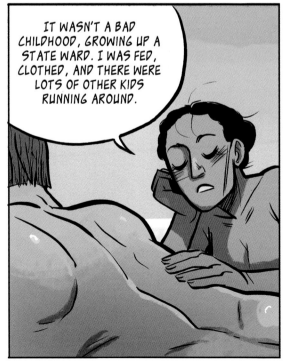

IT WASN'T A BAD CHILDHOOD, GROWING UP A STATE WARD. I WAS FED, CLOTHED, AND THERE WERE LOTS OF OTHER KIDS RUNNING AROUND.

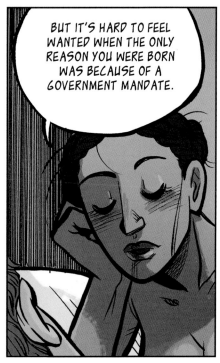

BUT IT'S HARD TO FEEL WANTED WHEN THE ONLY REASON YOU WERE BORN WAS BECAUSE OF A GOVERNMENT MANDATE.

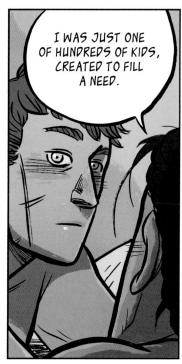

I WAS JUST ONE OF HUNDREDS OF KIDS, CREATED TO FILL A NEED.

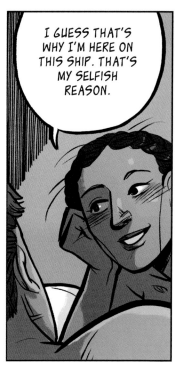

I GUESS THAT'S WHY I'M HERE ON THIS SHIP. THAT'S MY SELFISH REASON.

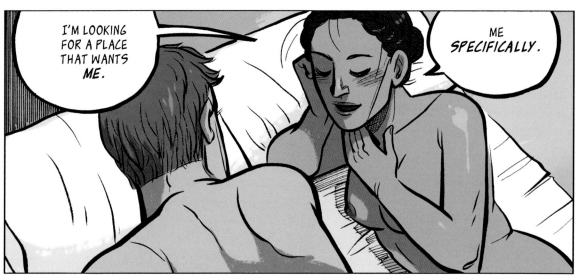

I'M LOOKING FOR A PLACE THAT WANTS *ME*.

ME *SPECIFICALLY*.

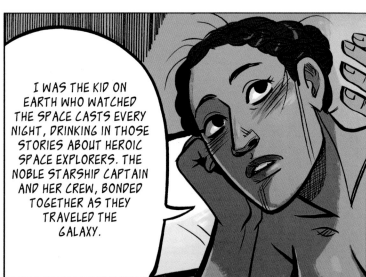

I WAS THE KID ON EARTH WHO WATCHED THE SPACE CASTS EVERY NIGHT, DRINKING IN THOSE STORIES ABOUT HEROIC SPACE EXPLORERS. THE NOBLE STARSHIP CAPTAIN AND HER CREW, BONDED TOGETHER AS THEY TRAVELED THE GALAXY.

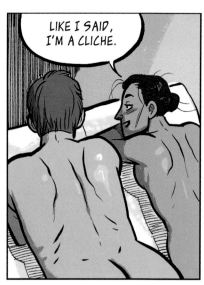

LIKE I SAID, I'M A CLICHE.

IT'S STILL A NICE REASON TO GO TO SPACE.
YOU LEFT EARTH TO FIND YOUR HOME.
YEAH. I'M GLAD I'M HERE.

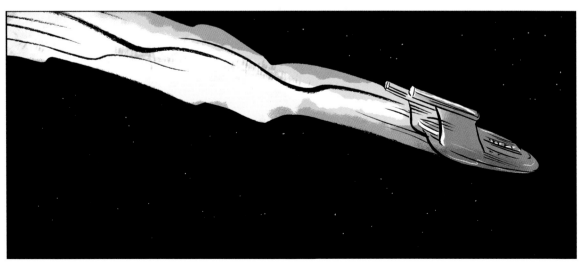

Amanda Lafrenais is a returning Iron Circus contributor, having work featured in **Tim'rous Beastie** and all **Smut Peddlers** to date. When not reppin' ICC, she is working on her webcomic, **Love Me Nice**, or erotic romance series, **Miracle Knight Remix**. You can find her on Twitter yelling about Sonic the Hedgehog.

amandalafrenais.com | twitter.com/amandalafrenais | lovemenicecomic.com

Anderjak is an artist based in Portland, OR. She's been making comics casually for what seems like forever, and professionally for the past several years. She lives with her partner and two jerk cats and will probably talk your ear off about game mechanics as narrative metaphor for three hours without stopping if you give her the chance.

anderjak.tumblr.com | anderjak-creations.tumblr.com | twitter.com/anderjak

Aud Koch is an illustrator who lives in Portland, Oregon and is a member of Helioscope Studio, the country's largest collective of comic book artists. She's illustrated comics for Dark Horse and Marvel, and done spot illustrations for Vox's **Eater**, **Strange Horizons**, and **Feminist Frequency**. She loves to read about and draw food, flowers, mythology, and quantum physics, and if you don't like salty peanut butter, you probably won't like anything that she cooks.

audkoch.com | twitter.com/audkoch

Blue Delliquanti is a comic artist and writer based out of Minneapolis. Blue is the creator of the science fiction comic **O Human Star**, which has updated weekly since 2012, and the graphic novel **Meal**, co-written with Soleil Ho.

bluedelliquanti.com | twitter.com/bluedelliquanti | ohumanstar.com